Barnabus Mudpatch

Street Knight of Waxminster

by

Steve Moran

With illustrations by the author

Also by Steve Moran

Jackie Potatoes
Starallax Revenger

To find out more about Barnabus and his friends,

please visit

www.barnabusmudpatch.com

You can also follow Barnabus Mudpatch

on

Facebook and Twitter

This book can also be found on

www.amazon.co.uk and www.amazon.com

both as a paperback and as an ebook for Kindle

First published by Waxminster Press in 2012
www.waxminsterpress.co.uk

Cover by Steve Moran
Illustrations by Steve Moran

ISBN 978 1 48187 005 4

To Bonina and Raphael

**Who fill my life with wonder
and fun**

Barnabus

Chapter 1

An Irresistible Temptation

Barnabus Mudpatch crept cautiously along the outside of the pavilion. As far as he could tell, there was no-one around to see him. The tall, striped, bell-shaped, tents were all quite close together, and arranged in long rows. The knights and squires were attending to their horses somewhere round the front, so there was no-one at all at the back, no-one to see him slipping inside this particular pavilion. He crouched down, crawled under the flap, and lay flat on the carpet, listening. There was no noise. No noise at all. He put his hand inside his loose-fitting tunic, and gripped his medallion.

"Thanks, mum," he whispered.

He slowly stood up and looked around.

He was inside a knight's pavilion, luxuriously fitted out with elegant furniture, including a huge wooden four-poster bed. But none of these things really held his attention. He'd seen expensive furniture before, when robbing the houses of the rich. No, what he couldn't tear his eyes away from was the suit of armour standing right in the middle of the tent.

"Whew," he whistled softly to himself. "What a beauty!"

He listened carefully. The silence was broken by someone talking far away, but there was no sound of anyone nearby. He stepped up to the armour, and stretched out his hand.

Barnabus had seen knights all of his life – from a distance – but he'd never been near enough to a suit of armour to touch it with his own hands. This was his opportunity at last!

He felt the cold steel of the breastplate. An involuntary shiver ran up his arm. He couldn't believe he was really touching it! He reached out with his other hand, and stroked the smooth metal. Then, unable to stop himself, he began to explore.

He leaned closer to the breastplate and sniffed. There was a cold, clear, tangy aroma of polished metal.

He could see his own reflection in it! His brown eyes were almost covered by a long fringe of thick black hair. He didn't like to see his dirty clothes reflected in the shiny metal, so he pressed his cheek against it and closed his eyes. It was cold, and incredibly smooth. Opening his eyes he stood back and looked at the whole wonderful construction. Every child knew the names of the parts of a suit of armour, and Barnabus was no exception.

The breastplate was joined to the backplate to form the cuirass. The gorget protected the neck. The pauldrons protected the shoulders and uppers arms, the couters the elbows, the bracers the fore-arms, and the gauntlets the hands and wrists. The faulds covered the upper thighs and the cuisses the lower thighs, connecting to the poleyns, which covered the knees. The greaves protected the lower legs and the sabatons the feet.

Barnabus could tell this was a suit of armour designed for jousting because of the roundels, the large circular plates of metal hanging from the shoulder guards, meant to protect the armpits from an opponent's lance.

The finest part, though, was the helmet. It was round, with a magnificent plume of red and gold feathers on top. It had a hinged visor which slid up and down, and which had vertical slits in so that the wearer could see out of it.

All of these components were held together by leather straps and buckles, cunningly concealed so that the whole collection of separate parts looked like a smooth, flexible shell of shining steel!

Barnabus Mudpatch was so enthralled that he'd forgotten where he was, and that he wasn't supposed to be there at all. Coming to his senses, he looked around the tent once more. He saw cupboards, chairs, a tall mirror, a table piled high with food, and a huge bed. Everything was the same as before, but he felt as if he'd been in another world for a while, a world where dreams come true. He let out a long, deep sigh. He'd never been so happy in all his life.

But, by rights, he really shouldn't have been there at all.

Barnabus was one of the Mudpatches - the children who live on the streets of Waxminster. But he was more than that - he was a Street Knight as well, an urchin who lived by a code of honour, modelled on the chivalrous knights he'd sneaked into the tournament to watch. Like them, the Street Knights were brave, but none of them were braver than Barnabus. He had a seemingly endless supply of good luck, and would never shy away from a bet or a dare. This time, though, he'd made the bet with himself. Not content with watching the tournament from the city walls, he'd bet himself that he wasn't brave enough to creep out of the city and sneak into the tournament grounds to take a closer look. Of course, he'd both won and lost the bet, so here he was, risking danger and punishment inside a knight's pavilion!

It wasn't easy to get out of the city because the officers of the Gate Watch saw themselves as the natural enemies of the Mudpatches, whom they considered to be beggars and thieves. So Barnabus hadn't gone anywhere near the gates, but had crept out of the sewers. That meant risking the Deadhand gang of course, but the east sewer was only guarded by Spider and Wagsnatch, whom Barnabus had fooled many times before. He knew how to get past them.

Once out of the sewer, he'd crept through the long grass until he reached the outskirts of the tournament ground. Everyone was so busy that no-one noticed him creeping around between the pavilions, and so he'd safely arrived at where he was now – all alone inside a sumptuous tent with a glorious suit of armour!

"You shouldn't be by yourself, my friend," whispered Barnabus to the armour, as though it was a fellow conspirator. "You need company, you do."

It was unusual to see a suit of armour not being used at tournament time. This was its busiest period. Either a knight was putting it on or taking it off, or a squire was polishing it, or it was seated on a horse with a knight inside it.

"You must be a spare one," whispered Barnabus to the armour. "Your owner's left you behind, just for me!" He had fallen in love with it. "You're beautiful," he whispered, and then slapped his hand over his mouth. He hadn't meant to speak. If anyone found him, he would be in enormous trouble. He whispered as quietly as possible. "A real beauty, that's what you are! And you're about my size! You must belong to the son of a knight!"

An idea entered his head. At first he ignored it because it was so ridiculous, but it refused to go away. The idea grew rapidly until he could think of nothing else. At last, it took him over completely. "There's no-one here, just you and me," he whispered. "Wouldn't you like a little bit of exercise? Of course you would! I know just the thing for you!"

Barnabus's keen eyes had worked out how the suit of armour was held together, and without pausing to think he started unbuckling the buckles and carefully laying the sections of precious metal onto the carpeted floor. It took several minutes to complete this process, and when it was done, the armour looked like the pieces of a giant jigsaw puzzle laid out on the carpet. The wooden frame it had been mounted on stood alone and forlorn, like the dried-up skeleton of a long-dead knight.

Barnabus had fallen under the armour's spell, and there was no way he was going to leave the pavilion without trying it on.

He looked behind the frame. There, on a table, were the underthings, the items of clothing designed to be worn underneath the armour. There was the gambeson, the quilted tunic worn as an undershirt. He picked it up, threw it over his head, and wriggled into it. The fit was perfect. Then he put on the quilted coif, the soft cap designed to protect his head from the hard edges of the helmet. Next was the hauberk, the shirt made entirely out of chain mail. That was really heavy! He put it on over the gambeson, and then put on the the chain-mail coif, a sort of flexible metal hood to go over the quilted coif.

He looked at himself in the tall mirror. If it wasn't for his dirty brown linen leggings and his old leather shoes, he'd look the perfect picture of a knight!

"You'd be proud of me, mother," he said quietly, raising his hand to his chest. The medallion was buried under the hauberk, the gambeson, and his own tunic, but he could feel it against the skin of his chest. He always felt happier when he could hold it in his hand, but that would have to wait until he took the underthings off again.

"Now for the rest!" he whispered to himself. "You first," he said, bending down and tying the sabatons over his shoes. The greaves were next, then the faulds, cuisses, and poleyns. His feet and legs were armoured. That should prove useful if a scorpion attacked him!

He wasn't sure what to put on next. If he covered his arms and hands he wouldn't be able to fasten on the breastplate and backplate, but if he put them on first then they'd restrict his ability to dress his arms and hands. What he needed was some help.

Up until this point he'd been concentrating so hard on putting on the armour that he'd blanked out all extraneous sounds. Now, however, something forced itself upon his attention.

He could hear sounds of activity coming from outside the pavilion. A voice of command was shouting something from a distance, and an old man's voice was replying from nearby.

"Yes, yes, I know. I'm going to get my master now. He'll be there, don't worry!"

Barnabus' sense of tranquillity disappeared in a flash, and was replaced by sheer panic. He was about to be caught! Him, a Mudpatch, not only in the tournament grounds - which was forbidden - but wearing a suit of armour as well! They might think he was trying to steal it, and then he would really be in trouble! The footsteps were just outside the tent. There was no way he could hide, as the pieces of armour he was wearing were just too bulky. Anyway, it was impossible to move fast while wearing them. He couldn't dive under the bed, and he couldn't creep out of the pavilion the way he'd come in. There was only one place left to hide. He bent down stiffly, picked up the helmet, and placed it carefully over his head. He stood up just as the owner of the voice he'd heard came through the tent entrance, muttering to himself.

Now Barnabus was really trapped. Trapped inside a cage of his own making.

Chapter 2

Mistaken Identity

It was an old man, with shoulder length white hair, and piercing blue eyes. He was wearing a red velvet jacket, with snakes and cockerels embroidered in gold all over it. Underneath it he wore a white silk shirt. He also wore red velvet trousers and black, shiny boots.

He looks too smart to be a squire, thought Barnabus, *and too old. Maybe he's the knight's father.*

The old man seemed surprised to see Barnabus standing there, wearing most of the suit of armour.

"Master Elvarin! You're up, and nearly ready, I see!" He sounded pleased.

Barnabus could see out of the helmet because of the narrow slits cut in the visor, which gave him a very limited field of vision. Luckily, they were so thin that no-one could see inside the helmet from outside. They were wide enough, however, for Barnabus to see that the newcomer was talking to him. He didn't know what to say, so he said nothing.

"It'll soon be your turn, so it's just as well you've started getting ready." The old man disappeared from Barnabus's view. He could hear the voice behind him. It sounded educated and deferential, but just a little bit irritated, as though the speaker didn't quite respect the person he thought he was talking to, but was supposed to behave as though he did. "Not bad," the old man said, appearing in front of Barnabus once more, but on the other side. "Not bad at all. It's not like you to start getting ready on your own, but I must say, you've made quite a good job of it."

There was a silence, as if the old man was waiting for Barnabus to reply.

I'd better say something or he'll be suspicious. But he'll know it's the wrong voice so I'd better not say too much.

"Mmm," he replied, as if he was agreeing.

"In fact," said the old man, leaning closer to inspect the armour, "you've made a *very* good job of it!" He sounded surprised. Barnabus could feel his fingers tugging at the straps and buckles securing the armour to his legs.

This gave him a moment to think, and one question came immediately to his mind.

Where is the owner of the armour?

He was obviously not here.

What if he suddenly returns?

There was no way Barnabus could quickly remove the armour and make a run for it. He was trapped. He would have to go with the flow of events, see what happened, and be prepared to take advantage of any opportunity that arose.

The old man was looking Barnabus up and down, appraising him with a professional eye.

"A good job, Master Elvarin, a very good job indeed!" he said. "I am surprised. And glad, of course, that something has at last soaked in. That memory of yours must be improving. Now, let's finish the job."

He doesn't think much of Elvarin, whoever he is. And wherever he is. Maybe he's run away.

The old man picked up the cuirass and opened it. The breastplate and the backplate were joined together by hinges on one side, and were open on the other. He manoeuvred it onto Barnabus, and buckled it into place. Then he fit the gorget around his throat.

"I suppose it must be something to do with that letter from your father. He never does pull his punches, does he?"

So Elvarin has a father too. I hope he's not here as well!

He said "Mmmm" once more, and hoped it was enough.

This was obviously the right thing to do, as the old man then continued talking. "I know I shouldn't have read it, as it was addressed to you, confidentially. Well, you shouldn't have left it lying on the floor, should you?" He was wagging a finger at Barnabus. "Personally, I thought he was being a bit harsh. Threatening to cut you off – you, his son, and heir to the title! – if you didn't make a good display of yourself here at the tournament. Up a bit," he instructed, and Barnabus lifted his right arm so the old man could strap on the pouldren, roundel, counter and bracer. Then he slipped on the gauntlet, and Barnabus flexed his fingers. It felt good.

"That's fine," said the old man, and Barnabus let his arm drop again. "Now the other one." Barnabus lifted his left arm, and the whole procedure was repeated.

I need to know more about this Elvarin if I'm to impersonate him.

He said, "Mmm" one more time to show he was paying attention, in the hope that the old man would speak again. The more he knew about his situation, the better were his chances of escaping.

"Just because you've completely wasted your life so far doesn't mean you should be killed. Well, not in my opinion, anyway."

Barnabus blinked.

Killed? Oh, mother! What have I gotten myself into?

He said, "Mmmm?" once more, in a questioning sort of way.

"Well, you might not be killed, of course."

Phew! That's some comfort!

"But jousting against those brutes might just polish you off."

Oh. Not so good.

"I mean, I know your father wants to toughen you up – and heaven knows, you are a lazy beggar, if you'll pardon my saying so! – but to enter you, a boy of twelve, into the Waxminster tournament, to compete against the champions of Gothria! It's just not fair, in my opinion. But I spoke up for you, I did. I told your father, 'If you want to send your son off to joust with the best knights, then you'd better buy him the best armour.' And do you know what he said?"

No, but I'm sure you're going to tell me.

Barnabus said, "Mmmm?" once more. The old man didn't seem to need any more reply than this.

"He said, 'Wildren, I'll buy that good-for-nothing son of mine the best armour in the land if you can make a knight out of him. You did it for me, so now you can do it for him.' Those were his exact words."

So, his name is Wildren. And he's some kind of knight teacher. Interesting. He doesn't look like a warrior to me.

"Hmm," replied Barnabus in a non-committal way.

"So he bought you this. I must say, it's the finest armour I've ever seen. It must have cost a fortune. I'm sure he has your best interests at heart, young master." Wildren was trying to be encouraging.

He wants to cheer me up. Well, it's too late for that.

"Hmm," said Barnabus once more, wondering what he would say when he was finally forced to speak. Still, the chatty old man didn't seem to need much more of a reply. At least, not yet. He was putting the finishing touches to the armour, and fine-tuning the tension in the straps by adjusting the buckles. There were no more pieces of metal left on the floor. Barnabus was finally dressed for battle. Then Wildren started to walk around him once more, making a final inspection.

I feel as though I'm in a prison cell that's just big enough for my body.

It wasn't a pleasant feeling.

I suppose I'm lucky that me and Elvarin are the same size.

"Yes, it should protect you from anything except a direct hit. Even then, you'll probably only break a few bones. Still, the other knights know it's your first time, so they are bound to go easy on you. Unless it's Sir Gratzenburg, of course. He doesn't have a kind bone in his body."

"Hmmm," said Barnabus, in apparent agreement. At the same time, his mind was in a whirl.

Sir Gratzenburg! That would be something to tell the others! Just think, I might get to see the one knight in the whole of Gothria who's never been knocked off his horse! He's a living legend!

His excitement was so great that he almost forgot his own strange predicament. Until Wildren spoke again, that is.

"So, that's it," he said. "You're all ready. And a very impressive sight you make too, if I may say so! Now, let's go. Stormchaser is outside, and you know how he hates to be kept waiting!"

That sounds bad. I wonder who Stormchaser is?

Wildren took Barnabus by the hand to direct him towards the tent opening, but Barnabus didn't move.

Uh oh. He means it. But I can't go out there wearing this. Someone is sure to find me out.

He was stalling for time, furiously trying to think of some way to get out of this ridiculous situation.

Shall I confess? Probably not a good idea. I wonder what the punishment is for a street urchin impersonating a knight? Execution, probably.

Wildren took his arm once more. "Look, Master Elvarin," he said, gazing earnestly into the visor of the helmet, "I've taught you everything I know. Just remember my instructions, and you'll be fine. You'll get knocked off Stormchaser and pick up a few bruises" - *Stormchaser is a horse! Me, on a horse!* - "but your father will be proud of you and will respect you at last. It's surely worth the discomfort. Now, be reasonable, and give it a try. Please Master Elvarin, just for me. Please?"

Barnabus could see the old man's face through the slits in his visor. He was looking at him so earnestly that Barnabus felt he couldn't bear to let him down. Elvarin – whoever and wherever he was – had clearly been a disappointment to the old man, so Barnabus reckoned he couldn't be any worse than him. If Elvarin was such a poor jouster that he was anyway expected to be knocked off his horse, then Barnabus knew that whatever he did, he wouldn't disappoint anyone.

Anyway, if I survive this, I'll escape when the armour's off me. At least I'll have a story to tell! And if I get killed, they can't punish me anyway.

That was not a comforting thought.

Barnabus tried to nod back to the old man to signal his agreement to go and fight, but he bashed his forehead on the inside of the helmet.

Ow! That hurt!

So he nodded his whole upper body instead, bending slightly at the waist. He thought he ought to say something as well, so he spoke in a whisper. He reasoned that Elvarin could be expected to be nervous, so Wildren would probably not be surprised to hear a strange-sounding quiet voice. "Don't worry," Barnabus whispered. "I'll do it."

Wildren got the message. "Very good, Master Elvarin," he sputtered excitedly, "your father will be proud. As will I," he added.

Barnabus tried to walk towards the opening in the pavilion that Wildren was directing him to. It was hard.

I must weigh at least twice as much as usual!

He realised that the only way to do it was to shift his weight from one leg to the other, in a curious side-to-side rocking motion.

This is like learning to walk all over again! If I lean too far one way or the other, I'll fall over sideways!

Wildren kept hold of his hand as they made their way out of the pavilion and into the world outside. Barnabus had not seen anything on this side of the pavilion yet, as he'd sneaked in from the other side. In fact, he could see precious little of it now, as the visor restricted his vision so much. He could tell that the sun was shining, and that people were rushing around, and that there were pavilions all around him. Then Wildren steered him to the left, and as he turned he saw the biggest, fiercest and meanest looking war-horse he could ever have imagined. It was like something from a nightmare.

Oh, mother, help me!

"I can't ride that!" he exclaimed, forgetting to disguise his voice.

Wildren didn't notice anything unusual. He'd obviously been expecting an argument. "Come on, Master Elvarin. Stormchaser is not the most patient of animals, you know," and he dragged Barnabus towards the most dangerous-looking creature he had ever seen.

Chapter 3

Finding the Balance

Barnabus stood completely still, and refused to move.

"Blazes," he said to himself inside the helmet. "It's as big as an elephant!"

He'd never seen one, of course, but he'd heard about them in the stories from the East, and this fearsome thing in front of him easily matched the terrifying monsters of his imagination. Except that this one was chestnut, and he didn't know what colour elephants were.

"Come on, Master Elvarin," insisted Wildren. "Stormchaser is only fierce to your opponents. He'll be as calm as a cup of milk in your hands."

I don't believe a word of it. That thing could chew me up and spit me out in the wink of an eye.

"Oh," said Barnabus non-commitally, as he stared up at the enormous beast. He was used to seeing horses in the street, of course. They were everywhere in the city, all the time. This creature, however, was something different, something special.

He's gigantic, and he's wearing as much armour as me! It must weigh a ton!

The only muscles visible in the gaps between the sections of the armour appeared to be bulging.

And his face – if it could be called a face! Stormchaser's mouth was pulled into a permanent snarl. Barnabus wasn't sure, but he thought he could hear the monster growling. It was hard to see its eyes under the heavy face armour it was wearing, but Barnabus thought that they were red.

This isn't a horse, this is a demon from hell!

A small boy in the same red and gold livery as Wildren was holding the horse's reins. He was visibly shaking.

With a great effort, Barnabus turned to face Wildren, and raised his heavy hand to point at Stormchaser. "Is it safe?" he asked, in the most plaintive voice he could muster.

"Don't worry, Master Elvarin," said Wildren, fussing around him once more, checking his armour for the last time. "Stormchaser won't move away as you climb onto him. He's much too well trained for that."

That wasn't the answer to the question Barnabus was asking.

Shrugging his shoulders inside the armour, he gave up. His fate was obviously sealed.

I should never have come creeping around, and I should definitely never have tried on this armour. It's all my own fault.

With a heavy sigh, he turned towards the monstrous beast again.

Is that smoke coming from its nostrils, or just steam? I can't tell.

Barnabus felt trapped. He was stuck inside his own personal, mobile cage. He was being forced to climb onto the most terrifying creature he had ever set eyes upon, and he was almost certainly going to be bashed around and damaged in a way he'd never even imagined before.

For a moment he felt fear. Deep, visceral, gut-wrenching fear. He almost blacked out. "Mother," he whispered, and he raised his gauntleted hand to his chest. It crashed against the breastplate with a metallic clang. "I wish I could hold you." His medallion was out of reach underneath an impenetrable wall of metal. Still, he could feel it against his chest. It was warm, and that gave him some comfort. It was just the reassurance he needed. It was something he'd felt before, something that came to him when he was in the most desperate of situations, like the time he climbed up St. Merrilan's church tower and couldn't work out how to get down again. Like the time he fell in the open sewer and nearly drowned. Like the time he rolled out of the way of the runaway horse and cart. It was the gift of his mother's medallion, and it gave him the strength to look danger fearlessly in the eye.

"I can do this," he whispered to himself inside the helmet.

"What did you say?" asked Wildren, unable to hear him properly.

Barnabus decided to take the risk. He knew the helmet would muffle his voice, so he spoke a bit louder. "I can do this, Wildren."

"Of course you can, Master Elvarin," replied Wildren, patting him gently on the back. "Your father will be proud of you, I'm sure of it. Now, let's get you up there."

Barnabus was glad that Wildren had raised the subject, because he really had absolutely no idea how he was going to mount this enormous creature. He felt the old man take him by the hand once more and steer him, rocking from side to side, all the way round to the other side of the horse. There he saw a small block of steps with a hand-rail attached, right beside Stormchaser. Sighing with relief, he ponderously climbed up the steps one at a time until he reached the top. Then, with a monumental effort, he lifted his left leg over the horse and plopped himself down onto the saddle.

"That's a relief," he whispered to himself inside the helmet. "I'm exhausted already!"

Immediately, Barnabus felt Stormchaser react. His ears pricked up, and his huge body seemed to pulse with energy.

"There, there," said Barnabus. He was too high up for anyone else to hear his voice, so he spoke normally to the horse.

Unfortunately he'd never been on a horse before, so he didn't know what to say, or what to do. He didn't even know if he should say anything at all, but it seemed like a good idea, so he did it anyway.

"There, there, Stormchaser. Everything's going to be fine." He tried to say it as though he meant it. "Now then, fellah, you and me are going to get on really well. I haven't done this before, but I expect you have, so I'm in your hands. Or hoofs, I suppose," he added, lamely.

Stormchaser snorted in reply, which Barnabus took to be a good sign. It was strange, but he felt really quite comfortable sitting up there.

At least I get to sit down at last! I had no idea that armour was so heavy. I suppose I should have expected it.

The saddle was huge and quite protective, with a high ridge both in front of him and behind him. It gave him something to hold on to.

"Your stirrups, Master Elvarin," called up Wildren from somewhere far below him. "Don't forget your stirrups!"

Barnabus hadn't even thought about them. He managed to bend his stiff body sideways so that he could look down, and he saw what he was supposed to do. One by one he manoeuvred his metallic feet into the hanging stirrups, and straight away felt more secure with his feet resting on something firm instead of dangling in mid-air.

That's better.

He decided to try something. Putting his weight onto his feet and pressing down hard on the stirrups, he heaved himself upright and stood up, gripping the front edge of the saddle tightly. Stormchaser snorted, but didn't move. Barnabus balanced carefully, and then dropped heavily down onto the saddle once more.

There's nothing to it! What was I so worried about?

The horse hadn't moved yet, of course, but at least he was feeling good about sitting on it while it was stationary. He'd always had a good sense of balance – walking on roof-tops and teetering about on walls, ropes and planks between buildings – so sitting on a horse was just a variation on the theme. Except, of course, that planks and buildings didn't move. Well, not much, anyway.

Just as he was beginning to relax, he heard a voice shouting. "Master Elvarin?" It was Wildren again. "I think you'll need these!"

Barnabus looked down. Wildren was pointing at a big wooden rack, on which was mounted several identical shields and several identical lances.

What the...?

Barnabus was confused. He raised his voice, and shouted through the visor. "All of them?" He was genuinely puzzled.

"Very funny. This is no time for jokes. Here." Wildren took a shield off the rack, and carried it up the wooden steps. On it was painted a snake and a cockerel, both bright red, on a golden background. Barnabus reached down and took the shield from Wildren with both hands. He'd never been this close to a shield before, let alone held one.

In for a penny, in for a pound. I suppose it might save my life.

He turned it round and slipped his right forearm through the leather straps on the back of it.

"Wrong arm," said Wildren in a long-suffering voice, shaking his head as he went back down the steps.

"Oh yes, sorry," said Barnabus, transferring the shield to his other arm.

"That's better," said Wildren, in the voice he would use for talking to a small child. "Save your right arm for this." He held up a lance. It must have been at least twelve feet long, and was made of solid wood. It was painted red and gold, like the shield. Barnabus took hold of one end of it with his right hand and tried to pull it up.

This thing weighs a ton! How am I supposed to hold it?

It was so heavy that he dropped it on the ground. Wildren picked it up and handed it to him once more.

"Rest it on the edge of the saddle, just as you did in the rehearsal, Master Elvarin." Wildren was shaking his head slowly.

Elvarin's father really can't like him very much. If I had a son, I'd never put him through this!

He didn't have the opportunity to reflect on this any longer though, because Wildren was poking him with the blunt end of the lance. Barnabus had no choice but to grab the huge thing with all of his strength, and heave it up onto the ridge of the saddle in front of him. He quickly found that if he balanced it correctly he could maintain it in a horizontal position, as long as the blunt end was wedged firmly underneath his right armpit.

Barnabus felt that there was something slightly ridiculous about his situation.

This is like being in a circus. I need the balance of the tumbler, the skill of the juggler, and the strength of the weightlifter. Still, I suppose I'm all right as long as I don't have to move. Which is bound to happen sooner or later!

It was then that he heard a trumpet fanfare blaring out from what sounded like far away. But then, with the helmet on, everything sounded far away.

"It's time, Master Elvarin," called Wildren. "They're calling for the contestants. We must go. That's enough of your joking about. You can't delay it any longer, you know. We're off."

Joking about? If only he knew.....

Without waiting for a response, Wildren walked round to Stormchaser's head and took the reins from the grateful squire, who ran away as fast as he could. Wildren threw them up to Barnabus, and by sheer chance they hooked onto the front edge of the saddle. As he had the shield on one arm and a lance under the other, he had absolutely no hope of trying to hold the reins as well.

I've got no idea how to control this thing. I'm just a passenger trying not to fall off, after all.

Wildren took hold of the bridle and tugged. Barnabus felt sure that the beast would bite Wildren's head off, but in fact, he did nothing of the sort. He did the one thing which Barnabus least expected him to do. He started to walk calmly and smoothly, as though this was exactly what he'd been expecting to happen next.

Which is probably correct. If he's a trained warhorse, then he'll know more about what to do in a tournament than me!

That was the last thought that Barnabus had for several minutes, as he concentrated extremely hard on not falling off.

The sudden movement of the horse was enough to completely upset his new-found equilibrium. Keeping his balance while coping with his shield, his lance, and his own armoured self was taking up all of his concentration. He quickly realised that to stay in the saddle he'd have to grip the horse with his legs, as his hands were fully occupied.

He also realised that the horse walked with a rhythm, and that the muscles of the horse's sides and back moved in a regular way. He adapted his own movements to match this rhythm, at least as far as his armour would allow. He was just starting to feel confident with his new-found relationship to the horse's movement when it stopped. He looked through the visor to see why.

What now?

He'd been so pre-occupied with staying put that he hadn't been watching where Wildren was leading him. Now he looked.

They were at the entrance to some kind of tunnel, standing still behind another armoured knight on his equally armoured horse. Beyond them came the sound of cheering, and then a smashing sound, accompanied by the whinnying of horses, followed by even more cheering. A powerful voice could be heard cutting through the noise.

"Sir Gratzenburg is the winner! Please remove the remains of Sir Valentril!"

That sounded ominous.

The remains! What does that mean? It suggests to me that someone's been killed!

The thought was not a pleasant one. It only then occurred to him that soon this description might apply to him, especially if he had to face the legendary Sir Gratzenburg!

Sir Gratzenburg! I don't believe it! I'm actually going to see Sir Gratzenburg! I wonder where he is?

He tried to look around, but his helmet didn't move much. All he could do was peer forward through the slits of his visor.

I'm in the tunnel.

The horse and rider in front of him had moved forward, and Wildren had led Stormchaser to take their place. From his new vantage point, Barnabus could see more clearly what was going on.

Stormchaser was standing in an archway which marked the other end of the tunnel. Before them stretched out the large open space of the tournament ground, long and narrow, with a barrier dividing it lengthways down the middle into two halves. The knights were at opposite ends of the barrier, and on opposite sides of it, facing each other. Stands were banked up on both sides of the tournament ground. There must have been thousands of people sitting there.

Blazes! I've always wanted to see this! What a fabulous sight!

The stands were decorated with flags of all kinds, and the nobility were dressed in rich and flamboyant clothes. It was a riot of colour.

The loud voice was shouting again, and the cheering was deafening once more. Then, with a resounding crash, the knight who'd preceded him lay unmoving on the ground.

Beyond him, on the other side of the barrier, strutted the biggest knight on the biggest horse that Barnabus had ever seen, even bigger than Stormchaser. The knight soaked up the adulation of the crowds as they cheered themselves hoarse, waving his shield and lance in the air. Both the knight and his steed wore jet black armour. The horse itself was completely black too.

Why do the villains always get to wear my favourite colour? Armour looks fantastic painted black!

The announcer's voice cut through the cheering once more.

"Yet again, Sir Gratzenburg is the winner. A direct hit has shattered Sir Boganor's shield, and probably Sir Boganor as well, by the look of it!"

The crowd cheered wildly again.

Why are they cheering? That poor man might be dead!

His thoughts were interrupted by the weedy voice of Wildren, struggling to make himself heard over the sound of the cheering crowd.

"Master Elvarin, I'm sorry, but I had no idea you would be facing Sir Gratzenburg! He was scheduled to begin the tournament yesterday morning, so he must have unhorsed every single knight since then! He is the best, and the worst, of them all! He will certainly try to hurt you, and the crowd just loves a knockout blow! If I may make a suggestion, Master Elvarin, I'd throw yourself off the horse just before his lance hits you. It will look to the crowd as though he's knocked you off, and although it will undoubtedly hurt when you hit the ground, it will certainly hurt far less than if he'd put you there! Good luck! Your father will be proud that you've faced such a formidable opponent!"

Oh, mother, no! Please, give me strength!

Having said that, Wildren stepped sideways, leaving Barnabus alone, on top of a savage horse, facing certain death at the hands of Sir Gratzenburg of Gratzlag, the Black Knight, deadliest warrior in the Gothrik kingdom.

Wildren

Chapter 4

The Ride of a Lifetime

Stormchaser stood calmly at the entrance to the tournament ground. As far as Barnabus could tell, he seemed to be completely relaxed, as if he was enjoying himself.

Maybe he feels at home. Maybe this is what he lives for. Well, I'm glad he feels happy, because I don't!

Barnabus squinted through the slits of his visor. The two stands-full of spectators were waiting expectantly. A hush had fallen. All the nobility were craning their necks to look at him, as though he was meant to do something. At the far end of the barrier, the huge knight in black armour was waiting, with his lance pointing straight up in the air.

It's not resting on anything. His arms must be incredibly strong.

That was not a comforting thought. Finally, something happened. It was the enormous voice of the announcer.

He must have been chosen just for that. His voice is really loud.

"My lords and ladies, the tournament is almost over. All that remains is to introduce a new knight to society. As you know, it is our tradition for the youngest and newest knights in the realm to face the champion of the tournament, so they can see what this new stage of their life will be like. Sir

Gratzenburg, will, of course, go easy on our newcomer" – a burst of laughter ran round the stands. Everyone knew what Sir Gratzenburg thought about 'going easy' – "so please will you welcome, at his first tournament, Sir Elvarin!"

There was a slight ripple of applause.

They just want to see me pulverised like everyone else who's faced the Black Knight! Well, he hasn't faced me before! Let's get on with it!

He tapped Stormchaser with the heels of his metal boots.

"Go!" he whispered. The horse didn't move.

There must be some way to start this creature! I wish I knew what it was!

Wildren clearly felt that it was time for something to happen too, so he slapped Stormchaser on the rump, and called out, "Go for it, Master Elvarin!"

Stormchaser understood this signal well enough. Without any warning, he leaped forward, and Barnabus almost fell off backwards, his shield and lance waving about precariously in the air.

Reacting in panic, he did the best thing he could have done – he gripped the horse tightly with his knees. This saved him from certain disaster, if not from complete embarrassment.

As it was, his shield and lance rattled and banged together as he wobbled along, and Barnabus caught a glimpse of the open sky as he was flung backwards.

The audience howled with laughter. It was a rare occurrence for a knight to fall off his horse before he'd even been hit, but this looked as though it could just be one of those occasions.

Barnabus heard the laughter through his helmet, and it stung him. He didn't like being laughed at, especially not by the rich. All his nerve came flooding back with his annoyance. He was Barnabus Mudpatch, Street Knight of Waxminster.

No-one laughs at me and gets away with it!

He heaved himself upright in the saddle, pulled his shield close to his body, and felt the balance of the lance resting on the raised edge of the saddle in front of him.

He gritted his teeth. Where was his opponent? Straining to look through the visor, he finally located him. Before he could focus, he was distracted by the announcer once more.

"Sir Elvarin, please continue to the starting line."

Stormchaser already knew exactly what to do, and stopped at a deep black line cut into the ground at this end of the barrier. He came to a halt there without Barnabus telling him to.

"Thank you, Sir Elvarin," said the announcer, in a patronising voice.

I'm going to wipe that self-satisfied sounding grin off his face as soon as I get off this horse. He's getting far too much pleasure out of me making a fool of myself!

The announcer addressed the audience once more.

"My Lords and Ladies, young Sir Elvarin is to face the Black Knight, Sir Gratzenburg of Gratzlag. May the best man win!"

Another burst of laughter ran around the stands.

Barnabus could see why. His opponent, at the other end of the barrier, was a hulking brute of a man. His shoulders were wider than his horse. Barnabus, on the other hand, was only a twelve year old boy, and not a particularly big one at that.

I expect I'd be laughing too if I was watching this.

Stormchaser snorted. Barnabus wondered if the horse could read his mind and was agreeing with him.

You're supposed to be on my side.

Another snort followed. Barnabus wondered if this was a question.

Yes, let's flatten him.

Stormchaser snorted again.

I'm so glad you agree.

"And so, without more ado," called announcer, "let battle commence."

It was obvious to Barnabus that Stormchaser was far better at this than he was, so he decided to give him his head.

"Stormchaser, it's up to you," he said. "Go on. Charge."

At the other end of the barrier, the Black Knight's horse had begun to move. It had started with a trot, and was rapidly moving into a canter. It would soon be a gallop.

"Stormchaser?" whispered Barnabus, urgently. "Do something!" Then, he took a huge breath of air, and at the top of his voice he shouted, "CHARGE!"

Stormchaser's ears twitched. Then, a feral snarl spread across his lips. His whole body began to tremble, and then, without warning, he exploded into action! His back legs hurled them forwards like some kind of catapult, and they were off.

Barnabus knew perfectly well that he was only a passenger on this trip. While Stormchaser was performing his duty as a fully-trained war-horse, he, Barnabus, was just clinging on for dear life, and trying desperately not to fall off. He had no plan to try and hit Sir Gratzenburg. In fact, he had no feelings of animosity at all towards him. The only thoughts in his head were to do with survival and nothing else.

I wish I could hold my medallion! Mother, protect me!

On the other hand, Stormchaser, a hard-bitten professional war-horse, was fully committed to the conflict. Unknown to Barnabus, Stormchaser had, in fact, declared full-scale war on his opponent! Looking straight at the other horse, eyeball to eyeball, Stormchaser was radiating aggression by the sheer power of his gaze.

Snarling and spitting, Stormchaser galloped down the barrier towards his enemy with death in his eyes!

Now, Sir Gratzenburg's horse – Crusher by name, a triumphant veteran of many such onslaughts – was not easily put off, but this time was not like any of the others. Horses know perfectly well that jousting is about knights hurting each other, and that they are only there to help them to do it. However, the sight of Stormchaser careering straight towards him gave Crusher cause for doubt about this philosophy, because he quite correctly sensed that Stormchaser intended him significant harm. This time was different from all the others. This time it was personal. In fact, Barnabus' war-horse was projecting sheer, overwhelming hatred directly at Crusher.

The effect of this was immediate. The sight of Stormchaser bearing down upon him was enough to make Crusher ignore Sir Gratzenburg's commands completely – which is exactly what Elvarin's father had intended by giving him such a fearsome horse – and as the two opponents approached each other at a thundering great speed, Crusher swerved completely away from Stormchaser, so Sir Gratzenburg's lance came nowhere near to striking Barnabus.

The crowd exploded into a wild chorus of cheers and boos. The cheers were from those who favoured the underdog and hated Sir Gratzenburg, while the boos came from those who'd bet money on him.

"Coward!" came one voice, cutting though the cacophany, quickly followed by a chorus of others. "Be a man, Gratzenburg!" "Scared of your own shadow?" "Lily-livered coward!" "Pathetic!"

To the audience it looked as though the Black Knight was trying to avoid Barnabus, while in fact it was Crusher who was trying to avoid Stormchaser.

Having galloped past Barnabus and Stormchaser, Crusher returned to his normal path. The Black Knight was fuming, and as he reached the end of the barrier he pulled on his reins furiously, and turned Crusher around.

Meanwhile, Barnabus had had a very pleasant surprise. He'd discovered that he hadn't fallen off at all, and was, in fact, still alive! What's more, he hadn't dropped anything – he was still holding his shield and his lance! All he'd had to do was squeeze with his knees for dear life, and try his best to stay put. Stormchaser had done the rest.

This horse is clever. Cleverer than me!

Stormchaser snorted, as if he could hear Barnabus's thoughts.

Much cleverer!

Barnabus was no expert on horses, but he knew one thing. Everyone liked praise. Even blood-curdling killing-machines.

"Well done, Stormey," said Barnabus out loud, stroking a rare patch of furry skin between the plates of armour. "You are brilliant!" Stormchaser snorted once more. Horse and boy understood each other at last. "Good boy! Good fella!" he said, patting Stormchaser's armour. The horse shook his head and whinnied, which Barnabus took to be a good sign. He was right. Stormchaser was slowly accepting Barnabus as his rider. Separately, they were each great fighters. Together, they had the potential to be an unbeatable team.

Thank you, mother, I'm still alive!

His hand rose to his chest, and banged against the breastplate once more.

Never mind. I'll be able to hold you later.

Suddenly, Barnabus was taken by surprise. Stormchaser was turning round! When he stopped, Barnabus could see that he was facing the Black Knight once again, but both of them had changed sides. Stormchaser had known better than he did what to do next. They were on opposite sides of the barrier from before, so their lances were pointing at each other for the second time.

His thoughts were interrupted by the loud voice of the announcer.

"My lords and ladies, due to Sir Gratzenburg's unwillingness to engage a complete beginner" - Barnabus could detect the scorn in the announcer's voice. That wasn't likely to make the Black Knight feel any friendlier towards him - "we will ask Sir Elvarin to kindly engage one more time. When you are ready, sirs, please commence."

Now if there's one thing you could say about Barnabus, it is that he's a quick learner. Adept at living on the streets, he was a survivor. He'd very quickly realised that Stormchaser understood this sport perfectly well. He'd also realised that the art of staying on a horse was very much to do with balance, and that if he was to knock the Black Knight off his horse, he'd better use some of his famous street-cunning rather than brute strength, not least because in that department he was seriously lacking compared to the hulking brute facing him.

There was no time to think all this through, but an idea was forming in his head, a very good idea….. and then Stormchaser was off! Not waiting for Barnabus to give him a signal, he'd begun his charge again as soon as Crusher had started to move towards him.

This time the Black Knight was not going to be caught out. Normally Crusher needed very little control, but against Stormchaser things were clearly different. Sir Gratzenburg held Crusher in a tight grip. There would be no swerving away this time!

Stormchaser was radiating aggression at the other horse just as before, and Crusher was just as terrified, but the Black Knight kept him charging in a straight line just the same.

Barnabus guessed that this time there would be no swerving, so he couldn't rely on Stormchaser to save the day. It was his turn to come up with something, and this time he did have a plan.

Everything depends on timing. And let's hope he doesn't realise what I'm up to until it's too late!

There was no room for error. The gap between them was narrowing by the second, and the Black Knight's lance was aimed directly at his heart.

Barnabus couldn't touch his medallion, but he could at least feel it bouncing around against his chest. "I can do this, mother," he whispered inside his helmet.

As they thundered towards each other, he sat up straight, pointing his lance forwards. Then, he threw his shield aside because he knew he wouldn't need it. The crowd gasped. Approaching Sir Gratzenburg without a shield was suicidal. Closer and closer they came, with collision inevitable. But then, at the very last moment, Barnabus swung his whole weight over onto his right-hand side, leaning completely away from Sir Gratzenberg, so that his opponent's lance passed harmlessly over him. His own weight nearly pulled him off the horse, but he hung onto the saddle for dear life.

At the same time, Barnabus swung his own lance round so that it was pointing sideways, at right-angles to his motion. This gave Barnabus a fraction of a second to give the great bulk of Sir Gratzenburg a sharp tap on the side with his lance as he galloped furiously past him. It was up to gravity to do the rest.

As Stormchaser continued his charge to the end of the barrier, Barnabus heaved himself upright. He didn't know if his plan had worked or not until he heard a loud crunching noise, followed by an enormous cheer. It sounded as though Sir Gratzenburg's enemies outnumbered his friends.

Stormchaser reached the end of the barrier and turned round, ready for more. Barnabus was desperately trying to think of another strategy, when he realised it wasn't necessary.

"My lords and ladies," bellowed the announcer, "I give you the winner – at his first tournament, the newcomer, Sir Elvarin."

There was another cheer, an enormous one, and Barnabus bowed as best he could while sitting in a stiff suit of armour. Now, through the slits in his visor, he could just manage to see the results of his handiwork. The Black Knight was lying on his side on the ground, unmoving. A cluster of squires were trying to revive him, but to no avail. The cheers continued.

"Come on, Master Elvarin," said the voice of Wildren, who was briskly walking round to the front of Stormchaser and taking hold of his bridle. "Let's get out of here before that oaf wakes up."

Barnabus was a little crestfallen that Wildren didn't compliment him, but he could say and do little as Stormchaser was led away.

Still, he would be able to tell his friends that for a few moments, he had been a real knight!

The medallion felt warm against his chest. "Thanks, mum," he whispered.

Chapter 5

Discovery

Wildren led Stormchaser and Barnabus back down the tunnel, across the field, and over to the steps which Barnabus had used to climb onto the great horse. Outside the tournament ground Stormchaser was a different creature. He seemed much calmer, as though his triumph over Crusher had vented his aggression. Or was it that he felt respect for his new master, after all?

Manouvering the horse into the right position, Wildren then relieved Barnabus of his lance. The shield would have to be collected later.

Barnabus threw the reins down and Wildren handed them to the squire, who'd reappeared, still trembling. Even a calm Stormchaser was a beast to be feared.

"See that he's brushed down and fed," instructed Wildren. "He's done us proud today!" Stormchaser snorted. He obviously agreed.

So far, Wildren had said nothing to Barnabus, who was still feeling disappointed. He didn't know it, but they'd ridden past knights and squires who'd looked at him with appreciation. The news of Sir Gratzenburg's defeat had spread like wildfire, so even those who hadn't seen it quickly knew about it.

What Barnabus also didn't know was how much the Black Knight was feared by all the other knights. Most of them had been unhorsed by him at some time in their careers, so they knew his strength and skill. That meant Barnabus was being looked at not only with curiosity, but also with a combination of awe, fear, and indeed, respect.

Barnabus ponderously took his feet out of the stirrups, rested his left one on the top of the steps, and slowly swung his right one over the saddle. Taking hold of the handrail attached to the steps, he pulled himself upright and realised that he was shaking. Then, he slowly walked down the steps while Wildren gave Stormchaser some water, which he drank thirstily. More boys rushed over at Wildren's command and tended to the horse, slowly and very carefully unstrapping his heavy armour. After all, his temper was legendary.

Wildren returned to Barnabus, and took his arm as he reached the ground.

"Well done, young master," he whispered. "It was, er, unconventional, but you acquitted yourself well. I think your father will be pleased when he hears you stayed on your horse." Then he added, in a low mutter, as if to himself, "although what he'll think about upsetting the Black Knight is another thing."

Barnabus wasn't listening to Wildren. He was concentrating on walking. He felt incredibly tired, and was getting sick of being wrapped up in metal. He noticed for the first time that sweat was running down his forehead and into his eyes, and he couldn't do a thing about it. This was no longer fun, but was becoming unpleasant. What had started out as a lark had become an adventure – and an exciting one at that - but now he was getting tired of it.

I want to go home.

That was all he could think of.

He was aware of Wildren's voice chattering away on the other side of his helmet, but he wasn't listening. He was concentrating on moving his incredibly heavy legs, and not falling over.

Finally, after what seemed like an age, he could see the striped pavilion they'd come out of. Wildren led him into it, and steered him towards the wooden framework the armour was normally mounted on. Barnabus walked up to it, and stood still. Wildren was still chattering, and he began to unbuckle the armour, starting with the cuirass. The breastplate and backplate came off in one large folding piece.

Barnabus froze with fear. He was trapped. Wildren would take off his disguise, and see who he was. It would shortly be obvious that he wasn't Elvarin. There was nothing Barnabus could do.

I've got to run for it. As soon as enough armour's off me, I've got to run for it. The old man will never catch me.

He braced himself for the getaway, and waited patiently.

Wildren removed the gauntlets, then the bracers, the couters, the roundels, and the pauldrons. Barnabus' arms and upper body were free of armour, although he still wore the quilted tunic and the chainmail shirt.

"That was a clever move, to push him off sideways," Wildren was saying, "but it's not one of the classical moves. He will probably demand a re-match so he can regain his honour, but I'm sure we can delay that until the tournament season is over."

Barnabus didn't care either way. He would be out of this armour, this tent, and this life in five minutes flat, never to go near a tournament again.

"I must say, Master Elvarin" - Wildren was on his knees now, unbuckling the sabatons and then the greaves - "I never thought you had so much imagination in you. You surprised all the lords and ladies of the court, I assure you, and they will be talking about this for years to come! I'm sure it will help us to find you a wife! They will … hello, what's going on here?"

Barnabus had been waiting for this moment, when Wildren started to notice his own poor clothes underneath the armour.

"Your leggings are rather dirty. I can't think why! In fact, they don't look like your clothes at all." There was silence for a moment. "…. and what kind of shoes are these, Master Elvarin ….?"

Barnabus knew the moment had come, but he was still wearing too much armour to make a successful run for it.

Wildren stood up. He had a suspicious look on his face. "I think I'd better remove your helmet," he said. "I should have done that first of all."

"Blazes, I'm caught this time, that's for sure," Barnabus muttered to himself. He was bracing himself for a fight, hoping he could overpower the old man without hurting him, when he was distracted by a sound. It was a voice. A boy's voice.

"Wildren?" The voice came from the tangle of blankets on the broad four-poster.

"Y-e-e-e-e-s?" replied the old man, slowly turning towards the bed.

Out of the pile of blankets emerged a head covered in red hair, followed by a body wearing silk nightclothes.

"Master Elvarin?" asked Wildren, in amazement.

"Yes, of course," said the newcomer in a tired voice, yawning at the same time. "Who else could it be?"

There was silence. Wildren looked at Barnabus.

"If you're over there," he said, nervously, "then who's in here?"

He pointed at the armour.

Barnabus began to tremble. Then the tremble turned into a shake. Then he was shaking so hard that his remaining armour started to rattle.

"Wildren, can you stop that infernal noise? I've got a headache, you know." The boy on the bed was holding his head, as if to illustrate the point. Barnabus could see enough of his face to see that he did look ill.

Suddenly, Barnabus felt an awful impact on the helmet which made his head ring. He keeled over, hit the ground with a crash, and lay sprawled out on the carpet. He groaned, and tried to sit up, but a tremendous weight seemed to be pressing down on his head. He couldn't move at all.

"Wildren?" said the lazy voice of the boy on the bed, "why on earth did you hit my armour? Don't you dare give it any dents! Father paid a fortune for it, and I'm going to need it today!"

"Master Elvarin, I have caught a thief!" said Wildren, angrily. He stood with one foot on the helmet, and a club in his hand. "A thief who was trying to steal your armour!"

"Really?" asked Elvarin, curiously. He crawled over to the edge of the bed, and looked down. "He doesn't appear to be trying to steal it. You're standing on his head!"

"That's to stop him getting up and running away!" retorted Wildren, sharply.

"You'll have to release him to get the armour off," said Elvarin, yawning again. "Here, I'll come and help you." He jumped off the bed and onto the floor. Then he knelt down beside the immobile Barnabus, and took hold of one of his arms, twisting it up behind his back. "I've got him, Wildren. Take off the helmet. I won't let him escape."

With his arm pinioned, Barnabus couldn't move as the helmet was removed from his head. It was such a relief to breathe fresh air and see daylight properly that he didn't mind his uncomfortable situation at all.

"Let's see him properly, Master Elvarin." said Wildren. "Stand him up. I anyway have to take off the rest of the armour."

"Up you get, boy," said Elvarin, twisting Barnabus' arm even more. He was properly awake at last. Barnabus got up with difficulty. "Now listen, thief," said Elvarin, firmly. "I'm going to release your arm so we can remove the armour. I'm holding a dagger in my other hand, so I can skewer you if you try to escape. No sudden movements. Got it?"

"Yes," he replied. He wasn't scared. He could run for it at any time once this armour was off, and the lazy lord wouldn't get anywhere near him with his knife. Wildren unbuckled the remaining armour, removing the poleyns, cuisses and faulds. At last, his legs were free.

"No funny ideas, mind. I'm watching you closely." Elvarin released Barnabus's wrist, and walked round to the front to face him. Barnabus was surprised to see that he actually was holding a dagger.

So he wasn't bluffing. I wonder if he knows how to use it?

The two boys looked each other in the eye while Wildren removed the gorget.

"Now for the rest of it," said Wildren, and he pulled the chain mail coif and the quilted coif off Barnabus' head.

"Don't you dare move!" said Elvarin. "Remember, I'm watching you!"

Elvarin had worked himself up into a real temper. Lazy by nature and easygoing by temperament, he rarely got upset. But the fact that someone was stealing the expensive armour his father had bought for him made him truly angry. He kept the knife pointed at Barnabus while Wildren removed the chain mail hauberk and the quilted tunic, revealing the dirty, ragged clothes underneath. Barnabus looked mucky, pathetic and very poor, like the street urchin he was. All three of them stood looking at each other.

They made a strange trio. Wildren, white-haired, elegant and annoyed; Elvarin, wearing nightclothes, aristocratic and angry; and Barnabus, filthy, forlorn and defiant.

"You guttersnipe!" sneered Elvarin, holding his knife under Barnabus' chin. He was furious. "How dare you dirty my armour! My father gave it to me for my twelfth birthday and now you've soiled it with your disgusting, dirty clothes! I've a good mind to kill you!" A drop of blood appeared where the tip of the knife pressed into Barnabus' chin.

"Now, now, Master Elvarin," said Wildren, who was looking from one boy to the other and frowning, as though he was trying to solve a puzzle. "Don't be so hasty! He was just, ah, trying on your armour. It's all still here, you know. No harm done!" He pointed to the pile of metal on the floor.

"I should hope it's all still here! It cost my father a fortune! He had the King's own armourer make it for me, exactly to measure! You, boy, are soiling the best armour that money can buy! I'm going to make you clean it, that's what I'm going to do! I've got to appear in front of the lords of the land today, so that armour had better be sparkling clean or I'll skewer you with a lance, you filthy street-urchin!" A thought suddenly struck him. "Speaking of which, what time am I on, Wildren? I mustn't be late, you know. It's my big day." Elvarin's temper rapidly disappeared, and he began to look extremely anxious. He withdrew his knife from Barnabus' throat.

"Ah, Master Elvarin, well, you see, it's a bit complicated. While you were…."

"What do you mean, it's a bit complicated? It's simple! What time am I on? We have to get my armour ready – and me, too! I've got to prepare myself! How long do I have?" Elvarin became flustered as he remembered what he was supposed to be doing today.

"Well, you see, Master Elvarin, you were due to meet the Black Knight. He was the last knight left unhorsed in the tournament, and….."

"What do you mean, 'I was due to meet the Black Knight?' Has it been cancelled, or what?" he asked, anxiously.

"No, Master Elvarin," said Wildren, softening his voice. "It hasn't been cancelled." Barnabus knew what was coming next. "To put it plainly, you've missed it."

Elvarin looked at Wildren in horror. The knife in his hand fell to the floor. He'd forgotten all about Barnabus. "Missed it? I missed it? I missed my one and only chance to joust in public?" He looked as though he was about to cry. "My father will kill me!" He collapsed onto the floor just where he was standing, and put his hands over his eyes. He started groaning.

"As well he might, should he discover that you slept all the way through your joust!" Wildren had turned his anger away from Barnabus, and was now directing it at Elvarin instead. Barnabus was confused and relieved at the same time.

"He was always an early riser himself, and never could tolerate laziness! Yes, Master Elvarin, your father may well kill you should he ever discover that you slept through your joust – but he won't, because of this street-urchin here, whom you were just threatening!"

"What on earth do you mean, Wildren? Don't confuse me! I'm confused enough already!" Elvarin's attention was now focussed totally on Wildren, so Barnabus began to have some hope that he might be able to escape.

I could run for it now, while they're arguing. But then I'd never know what happened.....

He eyed the tent entrance, reckoning that he would have to jump over Elvarin to get there.

"I mean, Master Elvarin," continued Wildren, raising his voice, and now looking as though it was him who was in danger of losing his temper, "that this street urchin has been out there in your armour, and beaten the Black Knight in your place!"

Elvarin was silent. He lay still, paralyzed with shock. Finally, he broke the silence, and cried, "Then I'm doomed! I'll be a laughing stock! I'm shamed beyond words!" He looked desperate. "I can't believe it! My life is over!" He buried his face in his hands for a moment, but then he looked up. "Wait a minute! Did you say he – he beat the Black Knight?"

"Yes," replied Wildren, simply.

"Not just any old knight, but Sir Gratzenburg of Gratzlag himself?"

"That's right. The most famous jouster in the whole world. Every other opponent had been knocked off their horses – by him, of course – and it was your turn to go next. This – this dirty street urchin, whose name we don't even know, turned up in your armour instead of you, and knocked the old devil off his horse." For the first time that day, Wildren broke into a smile. "It was the sweetest joust I ever did see, and how the crowd loved it!" His voice hardened once more, and he spoke firmly to Elvarin, who was still lying on the carpet. "You should be grateful to" - he turned to Barnabus - "what is your name, boy?"

"Barnabus, sir, if you please," he replied, quite happy about the way things were working out. *I'm not going to have to run for it after all!* "Barnabus Mudpatch, Street Knight of Waxminster."

"Barnabus? A fine, upstanding name, if I may say so." Wildren smiled for the second time that day. "And one of the legendary Street Knights? I am pleased to meet you, young man. Delighted, actually. And may I .....?" He held out his wrinkled old hand. Barnabus wiped his own grubby one on his tunic, and then grasped Wildren's clean one. They shook hands vigorously. "You know, my boy, I have seen the Black Knight jousting for over twenty years, and not once have I seen him knocked off until today! It was worth the wait, I can assure you! He was still unconscious when we left the tournament ground!" He released Barnabus's grip.

He's strong for an old man, thought Barnabus, flexing his fingers.

Elvarin was still lying on the floor, looking despondent. "What good is that to me? I'll be a laughing stock when everyone discovers I didn't do it! My life is ruined!" He buried his head in his hands once more.

Barnabus felt it was time for him to speak up. His moment had come, and he could see the way out of this mess, a way that would suit them all.

"Begging your pardon, sirs, but there's no-one knows the truth except us three and that big horse of yours, who thought he had a sack of potatoes on his back. He's not telling anyone, and neither am I, because I'd only get into a whole lot of trouble, and who'd believe me anyway?" He smiled at Wildren, and then at Elvarin, who gaped at him open mouthed.

In fact, they both looked at him in astonishment, as though they hadn't realised he could talk, let alone think.

"Nobody knows," said Wildren to Elvarin in a whisper.

"And nobody will know," said Barnabus. "My word as a Street Knight."

Elvarin looked at him, as if seeing him for the first time. "You really knocked the Black Knight off his horse while wearing my armour?"

Barnabus nodded.

Elvarin sat up on the carpet. "And you won't tell anyone it was you?"

Barnabus shook his head. "Why would I do that? I'd only get into trouble for being in the tournament grounds."

"So my father will think that I did it!" whispered Elvarin.

"Him, and the whole world," said Wildren, smiling for the third time that day.

"Then, my friend Barnabus," said Elvarin, getting up from the carpet at last, with a big, broad grin on his face, "I owe you an apology." He tucked his knife into his belt, and held out his hand. Barnabus took it. "And I hope you will forgive my boorish behaviour," he added.

"I've known much worse, sir, that I have," said Barnabus, smiling broadly.

"No, don't call me sir," said Elvarin. "We are the same size and age, you and I, and if I'm not mistaken, you're the better knight. Sir Gratzenburg hasn't been unhorsed in living memory, and for the world to think that I've done it is a prize beyond measure! I'm in debt to you, Barnabus, a debt so deep I doubt I can ever repay it!"

Elvarin was shaking Barnabus' hand so violently that his teeth were beginning to chatter. Barnabus managed to disengage his hand and say, "Think nothing of it, Elvarin, sir. I had the time of my life, even if I was scared stiff."

"Barnabus, my boy," said Wildren, patting him on the back. "You are a true knight. There is no doubt about it. Courteous, modest, and brave in the face of danger. I am proud to know you, my boy. And if there is any way we can recompense you ..."

Barnabus couldn't believe his luck. At first these lords looked as though they were going to cut his throat, and now they were his best friends.

You just never know with luck, he thought.

"Well," he said at last, staring at the table piled high with food, "there is something you could do for me."

Elvarin

Chapter 6

The Street Knights of Waxminster

Barnabus was clinging to the brick wall of the sewer pipe that was his main entrance and exit to the city on the east side of Waxminster. He was finding it hard to manoeuvre because of the heavy shoulder bag he was carrying. It was full of food. Elvarin had tried to give him gold, but Barnabus had turned it down. "Someone'd only think I'd stolen it," he said, "and it'd cause more trouble than it's worth. Some grub would be much more useful!"

Wildren was only too eager to reward Barnabus, so he'd filled a large leather bag to bursting point with all the food he could fit into it. There was fruit, a joint of ham, chicken in wax paper, loaves of bread, some pastries, and even a bottle of wine. Barnabus was delighted. His team would enjoy all the treats, and they should last for a week at least. What's more, he could sell the leather bag for a tidy sum on the black market.

Barnabus was never one to dwell on the past. Each moment as a Street Knight was full of danger, and required total concentration to avoid capture, injury, or even death. So it was that as he made his way back into the city through the sewers, his attention was focussed on the challenges ahead – how to slip past the sentries of the Deadhand gang, how to avoid the City Watch – and his success on the jousting field was rapidly fading from his mind. It wasn't in his nature to dwell on the past. He was more of a forward-looking person, anticipating the problems ahead, and solving them before they arose.

Which was just as well, because around the corner, in the next pipe, were the two sentries of the Deadhand gang.

Barnabus knew this perfectly well, of course, which was why he'd been creeping along so quietly. As he reached the crossways of the tunnels, where he knew the sentries would be hiding, he stopped. Putting his hand into his bag, he whispered, "Pssst. Spider, Wagsnatch. It's me, Barnabus!"

There was a moment's silence, then there came a reply. If a voice could be said to be slimy, this one was. "So, the filthy little street-urchin has returned, has he? He'd better have something for us, like he promised!" Another voice could be heard sniggering in the background.

Barnabus climbed up the brick wall as high as he could go. There were huge cracks in the old brickwork, so it wasn't difficult. He held on tightly with one hand as he carefully felt inside the bag with the other.

"Yes, I've brought you something from outside," he called. "I can't see you though, so you'll have to come closer if you want it!"

He heard splashing sounds as the two Deadhand watchmen came towards the crossways out of a side tunnel. He listened carefully to the sound of their splashing feet, anticipating their arrival at the junction of the tunnels to the split second. As their ugly faces appeared round the corner he gave them no time to think, and threw a loaf of bread at Spider and a bottle of wine at Wagsnatch. They were so eager to catch their presents – and so worried about dropping them into the filthy sewer water – that they hardly noticed as Barnabus leaped over them, and dashed away down the main sewer into the city.

"Hey, Barney, what about the rest?" echoed Spider's voice behind him as he ran.

"There isn't any more," shouted Barnabus, running like mad. Then he added, under his breath, "At least, not for you there isn't."

Knowing he would pay a price for his cheek at a later date – because no-one ever cheated the Deadhands and got away with it – Barnabus hurried along at full speed. If he'd stopped to talk to Spider and Wagsnatch they would have taken all of his food and the leather bag, too. He'd have had nothing left to take home to the children he was responsible for, but on the other hand, at least he'd have had no debt to pay to the Deadhands.

Oh well, I'll worry about that later. Now I've got to get home. They'll be wondering what's happened to me.

As his name suggested, Barnabus Mudpatch was a street child, living on the muddy highways and byways of the great city of Waxminster. There were a great many like him, living in the cellars, attics, and drafty back rooms of the city's derelict buildings. Always on the move in case the City Watch caught them, they looked after each other, constantly seeking out opportunities and watching for danger. Orphans and runaways, their ages ranged from toddler to teenager. When they became old enough to work, they left the streets to go and find employment. Some joined the King's army in far away Pendarion. Others became labourers or seamstresses, blacksmiths or carpenters, or started work in the massive candle factories that gave Waxminster its name.

Some became career criminals with the Snuffers, the Sparklers or the Brassnecks. The worst of them ended up in the worst of the gangs – the Deadhands, the mob that ruled the seedy underworld of the great city.

But the vast majority of the children of the streets were better than that. They were a proud and keenly self-protective band, a huge family of children with no parents. Many had come to the streets without a first name, so had chosen one or been given one by the older children. One thing they all had in common, though, was their last name. They were all called Mudpatch. It was a condition of belonging to the gang that they took the name of their new family. Living in the dirty streets and alleys, continually splattered with mud, it was an accurate description of their appearance.

Despite that, they were a proud and honourable bunch. They lived by a code. True, they stole in order to live, but they never hurt anyone – unless it was in self-defence. Nor would they ever bring dishonour to any of the other Mudpatches. Above all, they would never steal from the Knights of Gothria.

The Mudpatches lived in awe of the knights, and saw themselves as knights in training. The real Knights stood for all that was good in the world – courage, honour, chivalry, and the protection of the weak. That was why the Mudpatches called themselves the Street Knights of Waxminster. It gave them a meaning, a purpose in life.

The Knights were seen as glorious, as something to aim for, not least because they were impossibly clean. Their shiny armour contrasted so strongly with the Mudpatch's own dirty condition that they seemed like gods in comparison. Wherever they went, whether riding through the city or visiting each other, or congregating at Lord Waxminster's palace, with or without their armour, the Street Knights stared at them in wonder.

Of course, the best time to see them was when Lord Waxminster was holding a tournament, which he often did. On the fields outside the city walls the great tournament ground was laid out, and several times a year the great lords and ladies of the land gathered there to watch the jousting and the feats of arms.

The poor and the dirty of the great city were forbidden to go anywhere near the tournament, of course, but that hadn't stopped Barnabus. There was nothing that could stop Barnabus once he turned his mind to it.

After taking several more turns – and following a route only an experienced sewer rat like himself could possibly know – he came to a dead end, which is to say, a pipe fed by smaller pipes which were too small for him to climb through. He listened carefully to the pipe behind him. There was no sound of Spider and Wagsnatch. They hadn't given chase. It was more than their lives were worth to leave a post given to them by the Deadhand gang. It was their job to guard the entrance to the sewers on the east side of the city, and extract payment from those who passed in and out of it. Barnabus had only given them a partial payment; he knew they would want more. They always did. Their memories were long, and Barnabus would have to think of another trick to get by them next time.

Satisfied that he wasn't being followed, Barnabus began to climb. There were metal rungs hammered into the tunnel wall, making a rough kind of ladder. He climbed up them, all the way to the top, until he reached the grating which let in the light and the water. Standing on the topmost rung, he put his shoulders to the grating and pushed. As it lifted up, he grasped the edge of the road above and hauled himself out. He was in a dark alley, as he knew he would be. He replaced the grating, and looked around.

This was one of the many entrances to the sewer network used by the Street Knights, and there was always a chance that one of the Deadhands would be waiting to catch them when they came out. This time, Barnabus was lucky. The alley was deserted. He could hear the sounds of the road at the end of the alley, but none of its activity drifted down into this dead end.

Thanking his lucky stars that no trap had been set, he took the easiest way up to the rooftops – straight up a drainpipe. The heavy shoulder bag – only slightly lighter after making his presentations to Spider and Wagsnatch – affected his balance, but he was used to that. Carrying things across the roof tops was the only safe way to transport them across Waxminster.

Once he was on the roof of the tall building, he knew exactly where he was. The roofways of Waxminster were for the Street Knights what the highways were for the gentry – their principal routes of travel.

Every Street Knight started to learn the roofways as soon as they were old enough to climb, and it took several years to learn all the roofpaths across the skyline of the great city. The beauty of it was that the houses had been built so close together, especially in the poorer quarters, that it was often possible to leap from one shingled roof to another. And where the distance was too great to jump, generations of Street Knights had added flexible crossings, depending on the size of the gap. These could be ropes, poles, or even planks with wires and hinges attached, so they could be raised or lowered.

The houses of the rich tended to be more detached from the other houses, making them harder to get onto, so in the more well-off areas the sewers – also known as the underways - provided a better route of travel than the roofways.

In cases of emergency there also the houseways. This involved climbing in and out of the windows of people's houses, and was obviously more dangerous than the other ways. Still, when a Deadhand was trying to kill you, any escape route was worth trying.

Only one building in the whole of Waxminster was truly inaccessible to the Street Knights, and that was the palace of Lord Waxminster himself. Surrounded by its own high walls, it remained impenetrable, and was a constant source of annoyance to the children who saw the whole of the city as their playground. Even its sewer gates were barred.

None of this went though the mind of Barnabus as he stood on the rooftop, surveying the Waxminster skyline. The bustling life of the city was down on the highways below, but up here, there was peace. There was smoke, of course, from the innumerable chimneys, but he didn't mind that. The sweet smell of burning wood was a kind of perfume to him, reminding him that he was within the safe confines of the city, and not out in the dangerous countryside, where there were no roofs to climb onto, or sewers to hide inside.

From here, the entire skyline of the city opened out before him like a great map. He knew how to get everywhere, as if by instinct, although in fact his knowledge was the result of years of exploration. He'd had to be versatile to survive.

Barnabus' story was typical for an urchin on the streets of Waxminster. He'd been abandoned as a baby – by a mother too poor to bring him up, he'd always supposed – and taken in by the Street Knights. The only memento he had of his mother was the silver medallion he wore around his neck. They said he'd been wearing it when he was found. It was tied with a leather cord, which he'd replaced many times, but the medallion never left him. It was always warm against his chest, and it was a warmth that gave him comfort. The medallion must have been very old, because the image of a woman's head on one side, and the writing on the other, were very worn down. Too worn down to recognise or read. He didn't mind, though. He thought of the woman's face as being that of his mother, and he often talked to it. He was sure it brought him luck! After all, he'd never had any of the terrible accidents many of the other children had had, and he'd even survived jousting with a real knight without a scratch!

The thought of the joust reminded him of the food he'd been given. He patted the leather shoulder bag. The children would love this! They'd have the best party of their lives!

Without another thought, Barnabus set off on the well-known journey to his home. Running and jumping his way across the rooftops, Barnabus followed a convoluted route known only to the Street Knights. It took him to the heart of Wickward, one of the poorest quarters of the city, where buildings seemed to lean against each other, as though tired, but not yet ready to collapse.

Reaching a tall building, he climbed onto the roof and found a skylight. He opened it and dropped inside to find a dusty, empty room with no furniture and only one door. He knocked on it, and a tiny slit opened up.

"It's me, Barnabus," he said. The slit closed again, and the door opened. On the other side was another room, with a table, chairs, and several children of his own age, all of whom were armed with knives and clubs. These were the guardians of the entrance to the Wickward headquarters of the Street Knights.

"Hey, Captain, good to see you," said a big boy, gripping his hand.

"Watcher got, boss?" said a girl, relieving him of his bag.

"You took your time, Captain," said another, slapping him on the back.

"I know," he said, sitting down and relaxing at last. "You'll never guess what happened to me."

And he told them.

Chapter 7

The Captain Commander

Barnabus's life was a full and busy one, with its rhythms and routines, just like any other. The adventure of the tournament had made a good story, and entertained the other children for many days afterwards, but it was never more than a blip in the daily fight for survival in a big city full of predators.

Barnabus, at the age of twelve, was Captain of the Wickward branch of the Street Knights. His daily tasks were many and complex, but they centred around looking after the children in his care. As a Captain, he ran a team of scavengers on the street. Their job was to beg, borrow or steal the food necessary for survival, not only for themselves, but also for the Nursery. This was where the small children who couldn't look after themselves were cared for. The unwanted, the abandoned, the orphans and the neglected - the Street Knights never turned anyone away. Barnabus had been one of them himself once, and he was grateful for the love and attention he'd received. He was determined to play his part in caring for the Nursery.

So every day his team would go out into the streets of Waxminster. There they would steal from the open markets, from the shops, and from anyone foolish enough not to guard their pockets. They were smooth, quick, efficient, and hardly ever got caught. They had three guiding principles; never to steal from anyone poorer than themselves; never to hurt anyone (unless it was a Deadhand); and never to turn away a child in need.

The team Barnabus was Captain of was one of many, and each had a district of its own. While food was their basic commodity, they also dealt in money, jewellery, clothing and stolen goods. In short, anything that could be sold.

They were not the only gangs operating in Waxminster. All kinds of crooks preyed on the population, too, other gangs who were not so moral or so well-intentioned. They were the forgers, the graspers, the hoodlums, the confidence tricksters, and all the bad types which can be found in all big cities everywhere.

There was only one commodity that all these different groups were interested in, and that was gossip – what was happening, when, where and why.

And so it was that a strange rumour was picked up in the Slaughterhouse district. The Street Knights who worked that area heard it from a butcher, who heard it from a fishmonger, who heard it from someone in the printing trade. It was such an unusual piece of information that the Street Knights passed it straight up their own chain of command to the Captain Commander herself.

And so it was, on this particular day, several weeks after the long-forgotten tournament, Barnabus was called to the Street Knights' headquarters.

Its location was not common knowledge. Only the Captains and their bodyguards knew where it was. It wouldn't do for the Deadhands to know where the Street Knights kept their greatest treasures and held their secret meetings.

As a Captain, Barnabus knew exactly where it was. He made his way across the Brewery quarter to an old warehouse, which seemed to be held up by massive buttresses of wood that supported its sagging sides. Its shabby, run-down appearance drew no attention at all from those who had to travel near it. In fact, there was something sinister about it, something which made passers-by feel quite uncomfortable.

In other words, it was just the right place for a secret headquarters.

Barnabus climbed up a drainpipe, and onto the roof. All of the skylights were boarded up except for one. He opened it and dropped inside. He had to be careful because the room had no floorboards. They had all been removed, leaving only the crossbeams that they used to rest on. Through them, Barnabus could see the stone floor of the massive warehouse, at least a hundred feet below. Carefully walking along a narrow beam, he made his way to the door in the wall of this bare and dangerous room. Luckily, it opened outwards, but of course, he knew that.

Going through it into the next room, he saw a boy sitting by himself, slightly bigger than Barnabus. It was Growler. He always sounded as though he had a sore throat.

"Hiya, mate," he grunted. His casual greeting belied the fact that he was one of the fiercest fighters among the Street Knights, and was Captain of the Bodyguards. Barnabus knew he was being watched through several spyholes and secret viewing points, probably in the floor and the ceiling as well as in the walls. There was no way the Captain Commander would be left with only one bodyguard, even if it was Growler. "The boss wants to see you."

"I know," said Barnabus, closing the door behind him. "Any idea what for?"

"Dunno," was the hoarse reply. "There's rumours, of course, but I don't know nothing much. That's why you gotta see the boss. She'll tell you what's what." Growler scratched his ear with a knife.

"Yeah, thanks mate," said Barnabus. "See you later."

"Take care, mate."

Barnabus and Growler had known each other since they were babies. Their mutual trust was absolute.

Barnabus opened the door that Growler was guarding, and went through two more checkpoints, each manned by friends of his. Friends who were as tough as old boots, and would give no quarter in a fight. After exchanging greetings, they let him go through without asking any questions. The Captain Commander's business was her own, and no-one else's.

Finally, he reached the last door.

"She's waiting for you," said Brin, a red-haired boy with a scar on his cheek. He sat in a chair with his feet on a table, reading a large, leather-bound book. Brin was a scholar and an intellectual, and one of the Captain Commander's closest advisers.

"Yeah, thanks pal. Can I go in?" asked Barnabus.

"You'd better knock first, mate. You can't just walk in there." Brin frowned at him. "You know the rules."

"No problem, Brin. Will do." Barnabus stepped up to the door, and knocked on it three times.

"Come in," said a girl's voice. He opened the door, went through it and closed it carefully behind him.

He was in a large room, with a big round table in the middle of it, surrounded by chairs. This was where the Council of Captains met, which Barnabus attended as a Captain in his own right. It was decorated in a style that was the nearest to luxurious the Street Knights ever got. There were tapestries and paintings on the walls (a bit worn), and statues in the corners (only slightly chipped). This was a room designed to express status – at least, as far as the Street Knights measured it.

Sitting at the Council table was one person, the Captain Commander herself.

"Hiya, Barney," she said.

"Hello, Izzie," he replied, with a smile.

Barnabus and Isadora were the same age, and had grown up together, as so many of the Street Knights had. She was small, with long, golden hair and blue eyes, and was very pretty. It was hard to imagine that she was a ferocious fighter, and had bested many a Deadhand in their periodic street fights.

She was also extremely clever, which is why she was their Captain Commander. Isadora remembered everything and everybody. As Captain Commander, she had built up a network of spies throughout the city which consisted not only of Street Knights, but also of any and every kind of person you could ever hope to meet in Waxminster. She was respected and feared by people who had never even met her.

But to Barnabus she would always be Izzie with the golden hair.

"How are things going?" The way she spoke put him completely at ease, as though they'd only been chatting yesterday. In fact, it was several weeks since their last Council meeting.

He moved to the big table, and sat down beside her. She didn't seem to mind. "Pretty good," he replied. "My team is working well. We've integrated the three new youngsters, and they're fitting in fine. Hedlic is leaving us to be an apprentice dyer, and Dronna is going to learn to be a seamstress. The younger ones grow, and the older ones go." Izzie smiled. It was an old joke amongst the Street Knights. "We've had a few injuries, but nothing serious. We haven't lost anybody," he added, "not since Terrin." Izzie nodded. She knew what the Deadhands had done to him.

It was just another aspect of life for those at the bottom of the social scale in Waxminster. Street Knights could be arrested by those in the City Watch who were unsympathetic, or even injured or murdered by other gangs. On the street, anyone and everyone was considered prey by those who were stronger or more vicious.

"Well done, Barney," she said, in her soft voice. "Your luck is holding. You always were lucky, weren't you?" Barnabus blushed. Izzie didn't give compliments easily. "In fact, very well done. You're one of our best Captains." Barnabus was starting to feel distinctly uncomfortable. He wasn't used to this kind of praise. "You look after your team. You treat them well and you train them well. They all turn out to be excellent Street Knights. You know how to care for our family, and those you train know how to do it too."

Barnabus knew he was good and was proud of it, but he wasn't used to being told it to his face, especially not by Izzie. Not only was she the boss, but she was pretty too.

"I just do my duty, Izzie," he said, embarrassed.

"I know," she replied. "But you do more than that. You do it very, very well."

Barnabus couldn't take any more compliments, so he remained silent and looked down at the table, shyly.

"The question though, is this," continued Izzie. "Why is it, then, when you keep to the rules, and hurt nobody at all, that the word is out on you?"

"What?" Barnabus looked up sharply. "The word is out on **me**? Are you serious? I haven't upset anyone! Well, not any more than usual," he added.

"I know, Barney," Izzie replied reassuringly. "I've heard no complaints, no complaints at all. But the fact remains, the word is out on you. I've heard it from the best sources, and I mean the best. The Slaughterhouse gang picked it up first, and it came straight to me. I sent out a few ears, and they've confirmed it. The word is definitely out on you."

"But who?" asked Barnabus, confused. "Who the blazes wants me? And why?"

"The 'why' we don't know, but the 'who' we do." Izzie put her hand on top of his. "It's the Deadhands. And they're offering big money. Have you got any idea why?" She looked at him sympathetically.

Barnabus had gone pale. He was at a loss for words. "The Deadhands? I've kept out of their way for ages .... except a few weeks ago, when I made a fool of Spider and Wagsnatch. But it was only a little thing."

"Yeah, they're only small fry. Upsetting them isn't likely to put a price on your head of ten goldens now, is it?"

"Ten goldens? The Deadhands are offering ten goldens for **me**? You must be joking! I'd turn myself in for that kind of money!" Barnabus couldn't hide his amazement.

"No, I'm not joking," Izzie answered, quite calmly. "I'm quite serious. And if they're offering ten, they must be getting paid at least twenty. You must have robbed Lord Waxminster himself without knowing it!"

"But Izzie, if the Deadhands get hold of me, I'll be tortured, or even killed! You know that! This is the end of me!" Barnabus put his head in his hands.

"Don't worry, Barney," said Izzie comfortingly, "you're one of us, and no-one betrays family. I'm taking you off the street as of now, and Beric will run your team. I suppose you're happy to let him do that?"

"Yeah, sure," said Barnabus, brightening up, "they all like him, and he knows the ropes. In fact, he's the best lieutenant I've ever had. But what about me?" he asked, anxiously.

"You're going into hiding until all this has blown over. Don't worry, we'll look after you. I want you to go home, grab what you need, and then report to Oswyn. You know his headquarters?"

"Yes, of course. In Snuffbank."

"That's right. Oswyn will look after you. Only him and me will know your whereabouts, so there's absolutely no chance of the Deadhands ever finding out. When it's all over, we'll place you in another quarter of the city, one where you're not known. Does that sound fair enough?" Izzie looked keenly at Barnabus.

He nodded. "Thanks, Izzie. I couldn't ask for more. I don't know what this is about, but I'm going to find out, don't you worry!"

"I've got my own team working on it right now," replied Izzie. "What you need to do is keep your head down and survive. Got it?" she looked at him sternly.

"Yes, Izzie," he replied meekly. "Thanks." He leaned over, and gave her a peck on the cheek. Then he stood up. "You always were the best, Izzie. I won't forget this."

"We take care of our own, Barney. Especially you." She gave him a wink as he made his way to the door.

"So, to Oswyn's then," he said, opening it.

"Yep, to Oswyn's, just as quick as you can." She smiled at him.

"I'm on my way," he said, and went through the door, closing it behind him.

Brin was waiting.

"Everything OK, Barney?" he asked, holding out his hand.

"Never better, old mate," he said, gripping it.

"Glad to hear it. You take care of yourself." They released their hold, and Barnabus made his way through the rest of the bodyguards and the room with no floorboards to climb out of the skylight onto the roof once more.

He was scarcely aware of his surroundings as he made his way across the rooftops. He knew the route so well that he didn't need to give it his full attention. Instead, he was concentrating on trying to work out why the Deadhand gang wanted him so badly.

Then, he had an idea.

What if they're acting for someone else, someone with lots of money? What if someone told the Black Knight that it was me who beat him? What if Wildren or Elvarin let the secret out, and the Black Knight heard about it? They said they wouldn't tell, but how do I know I can trust them?

The idea gripped him completely, which was why he didn't see the net descending on him or feel the knock on the back of his head until it was too late.

Chapter 8

A Strange Delivery

Barnabus woke up with an awful headache. His hands were secured behind his back, his feet were tied together, and he was in a completely dark place that seemed to be moving. Also, he was gagged, and could only breathe through his nose. The air was permeated with the smell of candlewax.

I'm in a carriage full of candles! They've kidnapped me!

He struggled with his bonds. He quickly realised that he couldn't exert himself too much or he'd become short of breath, and, as he could only breathe through his nose, he might suffocate. He lay still, and tried to calm his breathing. The carriage – if that's what it was – rattled along. All Barnabus had to accompany him were his own gloomy thoughts.

His mind went round and round in circles, trying to work out who would want to kidnap him. Whichever way he looked at it, the only person with the motive and the money was Sir Gratzenburg. No-one else at all came to mind.

He wanted to hold his medallion, but it was impossible. Still, he could feel it lying on his chest. That was some comfort.

Mother, protect me!

He had no idea how long he'd been in the carriage. He had no idea where he was going. To find anything out he'd have to wait until someone released him. The only things he knew for certain were that his head hurt, and that he was hungry and thirsty.

His suffering seemed to go on forever, and he was finally beginning to drift off into a fitful half-sleep when the movement stopped.

His eyes snapped open. At last! Something was happening! He heard voices, muffled through the candles that must be above him. The wagon shook, as though boxes were being moved. They were uncovering him!

He tried to keep his breath steady, even though he was nervous. The sounds of speech came closer, as layers of boxes were removed. Finally, there was only a piece of wood between him and his captors.

When it was taken away he was blinded. He'd been in the dark for so long that his eyes couldn't bear the daylight. As he lay there with them squeezed tight shut, a slimy voice spoke to him. It was unpleasantly familiar.

"So, Barney boy, you're awake at last. How nice for you."

Barnabus would know that voice anywhere.

It was Spider.

Barnabus was grabbed and roughly pulled up from the bottom of the cart. He still couldn't see properly, but he could feel the hard candle boxes he was dumped onto. His gag was untied, and he gratefully sucked in great lungfuls of air. As his breathing steadied, his eyes became used to the light, until, at last, he could see properly.

He was sitting in the back of a large cart with Spider. Spider's white face was uncomfortably close to his, and was sneering unpleasantly at him. Wagsnatch was sitting in the driver's seat, sniggering and holding the reins, which were attached to two large horses.

"What's going on, Spider?" demanded Barnabus, after he'd got his breath back.

"You tell us, Barney boy. Me and Wagsnatch are being paid to deliver you, that's all I know. And, lucky for you, the deal is – no torture, no injuries. Which means, unfortunately, no fun for me and Waggie." Wagsnatch sniggered again. "But at least we'll get well paid, even if we can't cut you up a bit." Spider hawked, and spat a huge green globule out onto the road.

"But why?" asked Barnabus. "Why are you doing this?" Happy though he was to be out of the depths of the cart, Barnabus wasn't feeling very well. Being this close to Spider was not a pleasant experience. "And where are you taking me? Why did you bury me under all those boxes? I nearly suffocated!"

"Questions, questions, questions! Calm down, Barney boy. The only thing I know is that we're taking you to a *quaint*" – he emphasised the word - "little village called Blodrell Sonnet. Why, I don't know. You were buried under the candles so that no-one would see you, obviously! The Gate Watch might ask a question or two if they saw an unconscious boy tied up in the back of a wagon! So it's easier for them and for us if they just don't know anything about you! Anyway, that's enough news. Why don't you just shut up while I give you something to eat?"

Barnabus was confused. Spider was his mortal enemy, and yet he was offering to feed him. The world had turned upside down. Spider was a dangerous killer, after all. Plus, this close up, he was really smelly.

"OK, just release my hands," said Barnabus, "and I'll feed myself."

"No way, Barney boy," said Spider. "Your hands stay tied because I know what a slippery monkey you are. I'll feed you like a baby. Me and Wagsnatch don't get paid if we don't deliver you, so we don't want you running away, do we Waggie?" Wagsnatch sniggered again, this time a bit louder. "So shut your mouth until I tell you to open it when the food's ready!"

Barnabus could see an evil glint in Spider's eye.

It's not worth pushing him. I suppose I'll find out what's going on sooner or later.

And so he tried to relax. He would save his strength for the moment he could really make use of it.

And that's how the journey went on. Spider sat in the back of the cart with Barnabus, and Wagsnatch sat in the front, steering the horses.

Travelling so close to Spider was not a pleasant experience. First of all, he was ugly. He was completely bald, and his skin was as white as a sheet. He only had two teeth, and his eyes were a bloodshot red. He had big ears, no eyebrows, and he smelled of rotten food and unwashed underwear. He dressed in black clothes which were too big for him, so he resembled an oversized bat. Secondly, he spent the whole time muttering to himself and playing with his knife. He would cut holes in the candle boxes, and clean his finger nails again and again. He was so restless that it was impossible for Barnabus to drift off to sleep, which was the only activity available to him with both his hands and his feet tied together. The only time Spider spoke to him directly was when he fed him, and even then it was only to give him orders.

Wagsnatch was less annoying. He had a thatch of shoulder-length grey hair that hung down over his face. Only his nose stuck out of it. Barnabus had no idea how he could see at all. He wore drab grey clothes, and looked like a cross between a scarecrow and a haystack. As he drove the cart, he sniggered intermittently, as though enjoying a private joke. No-one ever knew what it was.

All the rest of that day they travelled, and when it was dark they stopped under a spreading oak tree. Wagsnatch attended to the horses while Spider prepared supper. It was some kind of stew, cooked in a filthy-looking pot over a fire that Spider made beside the road. When it was cool he spooned it into Barnabus's mouth until he was full, and then, when he and Wagsnatch had eaten, they all slept in the back of the cart in the furs that Spider had brought.

At dawn the next day they woke up, and after a breakfast of dry bread and water, they continued on their journey.

It was the middle of the day when the cart approached the village of Blodrell Sonnet. It was actually a medium sized town, built in a valley, with a river running through the middle of it. Overshadowing the village was a huge castle.

"That's where yer going, Barney boy," sneered Spider. "I expect they'll lock you up in the dungeons and throw the key away. That's what I'd do if I was them!"

Wagsnatch sniggered in the driver's seat. Then he whipped the horses, as if to show that's what he'd like to do to Barnabus. The horses took no notice, and just carried on walking at their normal, unvarying speed.

Barnabus was trying his best not to talk to the two Deadhands because all he got in reply were insults or threats, but he tried one more time.

I must find out if they're taking me to the Black Knight.

"Just tell me why we're going there! It can't hurt, now that we've nearly arrived!"

"You cheeky young dog!" snarled Spider, raising his hand to strike Barnabus. He held himself back at the last minute. "Always asking questions! You're lucky I don't whip you, you nuisance! It's our job, that's all! The gang is paying us to do this – it's not like we have any choice anyway – and we got given the job 'cos we know you! The way you cheeked us in the sewers, how could we forget? So we got told to take you to the middle of nowhere, and miss all the fun in the city. We ain't doing this for fresh air, it's 'cos we've gotta do it. It's a

Deadhand contract, you see. When the gang tells us to jump, we jump. And you'd be jumping at the end of my whip too, boy, if the contract hadn't said to deliver you in good condition. I expect they want to torture you themselves, that's what it'll be, and not have us spoil it for them! Ha ha ha!"

Spider's evil cackle and Wagsnatch's insidious snigger echoed across the valley. Barnabus could see no more point in talking to these two thugs, so he kept quiet.

They don't know anything. Whether it's the Black Knight or not, this is the end of me. I'm sorry, mother. I wish I'd made more of my life.

The only noises to be heard as the cart made its last trek from the countryside into the village of Blodrell Sonnet were the sounds of the birds singing, the wind blowing, and Wagsnatch quietly sniggering to himself.

Chapter 9

The Mystery Solved

The cart wound its way through the streets of Blodrell Sonnet. Wagsnatch was driving, and Spider sat in the back of the wagon with Barnabus. They both sat on candle boxes, but Barnabus was covered with furs so that no-one could see his hands and feet tied together.

Spider was not happy. First of all, he'd left Waxminster, something he didn't like to do. Secondly, he knew that the Deadhands had spies everywhere. If Barnabus looked even a little bit damaged, he, Spider, would get into serious trouble. If he escaped before the handover, Spider and Wagsnatch would not get paid. Worse than that, they would be punished for letting the merchandise get away and not fulfilling the contract.

Barnabus, on the other hand, was excited. As long as he didn't dwell on his uncertain future, he was enjoying being outside of the great city. Everything was new, and different from what he was used to. He looked around eagerly at the buildings and shops of this village, which was much smaller than Waxminster. In fact, it was so much smaller that the air smelled clean even in the main street. Barnabus reckoned that this whole village would easily fit inside his own district of Wickward. That would make it harder to hide, should he escape, of course. Such a small place would be very easy to search. Nevertheless, he did his best to memorise the layout of the village. Shops, inns, stables, all of them were landmarks that he quickly committed to memory. Spider and Wagsnatch may well have an agreement with the Deadhand gang to deliver him unharmed, but he had no idea whatsoever about the intentions of the Black Knight, or whoever he was being delivered to. As soon as he could escape, he would, and stow himself away in a wagon going back to Waxminster.

For a moment he reflected on Izzie's promise to keep him safe, and how useless it had been. But as he'd been captured before he could even go into hiding, he could hardly blame the Captain Commander of the Street Knights.

If I know Izzie, she's already turning Waxminster upside down looking for me.

His daydreaming came to a halt as the wagon stopped with a jolt. They were outside a seedy and decrepit-looking building, and Wagsnatch tied up the horses while Spider cut the rope which tied Barnabus's ankles together. He stretched his legs. It felt good. Spider hauled him up onto his feet, and he shuffled to the back of the wagon. Spider jumped down onto the ground, and reached up. He grabbed hold of Barnabus, and lifted him down as well.

"Don't try anything, Barney boy," muttered Spider. "I've got a knife in me hand. And don't think I don't know how to use it!" Then he cut the ropes binding Barnabus' wrists, spun him round, and pressed the point of the knife into his back.

Wagsnatch came round to the back of the wagon, pointed at the building, and grunted.

"I think you're right, Waggie. This is the place," replied Spider.

Above the door of the building was an old, faded, weatherbeaten sign. "Snake and Cockerel," it said. This was obviously an inn, and a run-down one at that.

"Now, Barney boy, this here hostelry is where Waggie and I are going to leave you. This is our delivery place. So, just remember, whoever we hand you over to, you say we've been nice to you, and no violence or nothing, OK? You understand? It's true, we ain't roughed you up at all, have we?"

"All right," said Barnabus. He would have agreed to anything to get this over with and be free of Spider and Wagsnatch. Little though he liked his captors, he had to admit that they hadn't hurt him. Apart from knocking him out in the first place, of course, but that was normal for a kidnap, and couldn't be counted against them. "It hasn't been cosy, but you haven't hurt me, I suppose," he admitted, grudgingly.

"Just remember to say that when we turns you in. Now, Waggie goes in front, and then you, and then me. Straight in through the front door, like. Got it?"

"Yes," said Barnabus. "I'm not stupid."

"Well, let's go then."

Spider poked Barnabus in the back with his knife, and they followed Wagsnatch through the open door into the dimly lit interior.

Once Spider was inside, the door slammed shut behind him, and the window shutters were rapidly closed, too. The room suddenly became very dark.

"And what can we do for you?" growled a deep voice.

The darkness was so sudden that at first Barnabus couldn't see anything. Gradually, as his eyes adjusted, he became accustomed to the dim light. Then he could pick out the shapes of figures standing all around them. Men. Big men.

"Now then," said Spider, in a wheedling voice, "no need for any aggravation, fellers. We're just making a delivery, so if you'll give me my token we'll be on our way and leave you to it."

"And who might you be, and what are you delivering?" said the deep voice once more.

"Now then, gents, lets not play games. I'm Spider, and this here is Wagsnatch. We've come all the way from Waxminster to deliver this young laddy to.....to," Spider had to concentrate for a moment, "to a Mister Silas Hackleberry, at this inn, the Snake and Cockerel. And this lad's name is ...."

"Enough!" interrupted a different voice, a gruff one. "We'll hear from the delivery who he is. Sonny, say yer piece."

Barnabus looked around. There was no hope of escape, and he had the feeling that lies and subterfuge would lead to more trouble than telling the truth. The Black Knight could always torture a confession out of him, anyway. He decided to go for honesty.

"Barnabus Mudpatch," he said proudly, standing up straight. "Street Knight of Waxminster."

"Very well," said the gruff voice. "Consider yer delivery made. Leave him here lads, and be on yer way."

"Aren't you forgetting something, mate?" said Spider, anxiously.

"Like what?"

"The token. You know, it's in the terms of the contract. You've got to give me the token the Deadhands gave you!"

"I've lost it. Sorry lads, it's time to go." The voice didn't sound sorry at all.

"Now look here, mate. You know as well as I do that they'll kill us if we go back without the token. Be reasonable lads, you know the terms." Spider was sounding desperate. Even Wagsnatch was starting to snuffle a bit.

"It depends," said the gruff voice once more.

"On what?" asked Spider, hopefully.

"On how well you treated the boy. Did they beat you, lad?"

"No, sir," answered Barnabus, truthfully.

"Did they treat you well?"

"Well, yes, I suppose they did, sir," replied Barnabus again.

"And did they give you enough to eat?"

"Well, yes sir." Barnabus could have wished for better tasting food, but he did at least have enough of it.

"That's all right, then. You can have the token." Spider gave an audible sigh of relief as he felt the token pressed into his hand. Wagsnatch gurgled.

"Thanks, pal," said Spider. "Can we go now?"

"You can go," said the gruff voice. "Just turn around first."

Spider and Wagsnatch turned around to face the door. Before they had time to think, the door opened, and they were pushed through. Both of them fell on the ground outside, and the door slammed shut behind them.

Spider looked at the token he'd been given. It was a small hand, black in colour, carved out of bone.

"Thank Sersei," he said, and picked himself up from the floor. Wagsnatch did the same, and dusted himself down. "Now we can go home!" Wagsnatch grunted in reply. He went to untie the horses, while Spider climbed into the wagon.

"If I ever see that Barney back in Waxminster, I'll give him what for, I will!" complained Spider. Wagsnatch sniggered. "Let's be on our way!"

Wagsnatch clambered up into the driver's seat, and cracked his whip. The horses began the long journey back to Waxminster.

Meanwhile, back inside the Snake and Cockerel, Barnabus was wondering if he shouldn't have returned to Waxminster with Spider and Wagsnatch. He was in a dark room, surrounded by large men. At least he knew where he was with Spider and Wagsnatch. With these men, he had no idea at all.

When will Sir Gratzenburg appear?

"So," said Barnabus brightly, pretending to be confident, "what happens now?"

The gruff voice spoke again. "My name is Silas Hackleberry. I run the gang here in Blodrell Sonnet. We're called the Blodrell Bloodhounds. I'm the one who contacted the Deadhands and had you brought here. Pleased to meet you, Barnabus."

"Pleased to meet you too, sir," said Barnabus, in as calm a voice as he could manage.

The voice spoke once more. "OK, boys, back to normal."

Barnabus felt strong hands seize him by the shoulders, and spin him round vigorously. While he was regaining his balance, the room changed completely. It took place so quickly that he was unable to see how it happened. All he could tell was that the room erupted into activity, and in only a few seconds the shutters had opened, tankards appeared on tables, customers were sitting on benches, and an innkeeper stood behind the bar, polishing bottles.

Barnabus had the strangest feeling, as though he'd been asleep for some time and had suddenly woken up. He looked around for the fearsome crew who had terrorised Spider and Wagsnatch, but saw only farmers, tradesmen and shopkeepers enjoying their lunchtime tankard of beer.

And which one of them was Silas Hackleberry, their leader?

He felt a tap on his shoulder, and rapidly turned round.

"Ah, Master Barnabus," said a familiar voice. "I trust you are well?"

It wasn't the Black Knight at all. It was Wildren.

Lord Blodrell

Chapter 10

A Surprise Request

"You see, Silas and I are old friends," said Wildren, as he and Barnabus made their way on foot through the winding streets of the village. "His father and my father had neighbouring farms. So we hunted together, played together, swam and poached together. Our fathers then directed us in quite different professions, but we always kept in touch."

"But he's a…a....a.…" began Barnabus.

"No, he's not," said Wildren, firmly. "He's not a robber, nor a thief. He is the unofficial protector of Blodrell Sonnet, and is the leader of the nearest thing we have to the City Watch. Or the Street Knights of Waxminster, for that matter. We call them the Blodrell Bloodhounds. So he is a colleague of yours, really."

"Oh," said Barnabus, puzzled. "But he deals with the Deadhands, doesn't he? No friend of mine would do that!"

"Only because I asked him to," said Wildren. "How else was I to find you? You left me with no address, so I had to resort to less conventional methods. I asked Silas if he knew any way of finding you and bringing you here, and he did. And here you are indeed!" Wildren finished with a little bow to Barnabus.

"So you paid him? And he paid the Deadhands?" asked Barnabus, incredulously.

"Of course," replied Wildren. "Well, not me personally. It was Lord Blodrell, actually, at my request. He's not short of money, you know!"

"He isn't?" asked Barnabus, incredulously. The idea was a strange one to him.

"I should think not! Look at his home!" Wildren pointed to the castle on the hill which dominated the village. It was larger than anything Barnabus had seen in Waxminster, except for Lord Waxminster's palace and the Minster itself.

Barnabus was overwhelmed to think that someone would pay the Deadhands to find him and bring him here. And pay so much! He felt guilty that such a lot had been spent on him. He only hoped he was worth it!

He was lost in thought as he and Wildren walked out of Blodrell Sonnet and up the wide road that led to the castle. His mind was in turmoil. His fury and resentment at being captured by the Deadhands were rapidly disappearing as he tried to digest the fact that Wildren had instigated it. Grudgingly he admitted to himself that Spider and Wagsnatch had not actually hurt him. They'd even fed him, and kept him warm at night, which is the very least that he would have done himself, even for an enemy.

When he thought of what they could have done to him – and, indeed, what the Deadhands usually did do to their captors – he realised that, in fact, he had come out of this whole escapade really quite well – at least, so far. And the result was that he was with friends! Well, with at least one friend, Wildren.

His mind was buzzing with thoughts, but one single question stood out above all the others.

"But what do you want me for, Wildren? You're rich, and I'm just a street kid! Why did you spend all that money bringing me here? I mean, I could've fed the Street Knights for years with the money you paid to kidnap me!"

There was another silence as they walked side by side along the wide road. Wildren was trying to think of the best way to say what was on his mind. Then, he spoke. "Barnabus, my friend. You are an unusual boy. Something of a special boy, in fact. You are a street urchin, well versed in the strategies of survival in the alleys of Waxminster. What is more, you are a Street Knight, so you have an ethic, a standard you live by. You care for those younger than you, and those in need. But even more than that, you are capable of dealing with extraordinary challenges with no preparation whatsoever, and overcoming them successfully."

Barnabus was puzzled. "What on earth are you talking about?" he asked.

"There is the little matter of you riding in a tournament and unhorsing the most successful jouster the Gothrik kingdom has ever known," replied Wildren, seriously.

"Oh, that," replied Barnabus, without much interest. "That was a fluke. I'd forgotten all about it."

"No, it wasn't a fluke," insisted Wildren. "It was a rapid and well-measured response to a challenging and dangerous situation. You are a natural and talented warrior, my boy. No adult – however experienced – has ever done what you did when you unseated Sir Gratzenburg. You can be proud of your achievement, and respect yourself for what you are – a talented young man. Quick witted, nimble, courageous and daring. A valuable ally, and a dangerous foe, I should think." Wildren smiled at Barnabus, and patted him on the back.

Barnabus didn't know what to say. He'd never received so many compliments in his life. Even Izzie hadn't gone that far. He couldn't deny anything Wildren had said, though. It was true that he was known among the Street Knights for taking risks – he would always climb higher than anyone else, or balance on the thinnest wall or pipe, if he was challenged to. He was also the quickest runner of them all, and the bravest in the face of danger, although he never thought of it quite like that. Only last week he'd dived under a moving carriage to rescue Anna from certain death, and – well, it was just what he did. He wasn't trying to show off. He could never think of himself as a hero.

"Well, so what?" he replied, belligerently. He was feeling embarrassed by so much praise. "Did you pay the Deadhands a fortune to bring me all the way out here just so you could flatter me? I don't think so! What's really going on, Wildren?"

Barnabus had turned the tables. It was time for Wildren to look uncomfortable, and he avoided answering the question. "Well, Master Barnabus, I think it is for Master Elvarin to tell you that. Come, we'll soon be with him."

Wildren and Barnabus had reached the end of the road. Immediately in front of them was the drawbridge which crossed the wide moat surrounding Castle Blodrell. Barnabus gazed down into the water below. It looked deep. They walked over the drawbridge, and were met by two guards wearing the Blodrell coat of arms, a snake and a cockerel.

"Master Wildren," said the first of the two guardsmen, bowing his head respectfully. "Welcome back." He had a thick, foreign accent. He was tall, with long, grey hair tied back in a ponytail under a steel helmet. He had a bushy grey moustache, drooping down on either side of his mouth.

"Ah, Captain Draxa," replied Wildren. "I'd like you to meet Barnabus. He is a friend of Master Elvarin, and will be staying with us for – well, for quite a while. Later on, I will be asking you to show him around. Barnabus, this is Draxa, captain of the castle guard. He reports directly to Lord Blodrell, so he's an important man to be friends with!"

Although Wildren was smiling, Barnabus could tell that he meant what he said, and that he expected Barnabus to take him seriously. Barnabus hadn't survived as long as he had on the streets of Waxminster without being able to read people's intentions.

He looked at the stern warrior, encased in chain mail, leaning on his huge sword. "It's an honour to meet you, Captain Draxa," said Barnabus, bowing low at the waist, and keeping his voice as respectful as possible. He remained bowed until Captain Draxa spoke to him.

"Well met, Master Barnabus. I am at the service of any friend of Master Elvarin's. Please let me know how I may be of service."

Barnabus straightened up, but before he could speak, Wildren interjected, "Thank you, Captain Draxa. Rest assured, I will be calling on you presently."

The Captain bowed his head again, and Wildren ushered Barnabus into the castle.

Castle Blodrell looked as though it had been built at a time when war was more common than it is now. The tall outer walls were interspersed with enormous cylindrical towers peppered with arrow slits. Any invader that managed to cross the wide moat would be met by falling stones, boiling oil, and a hail of arrows.

The walls reached all the way round the castle, enclosing an area as big as a small town. The principle building inside was the Keep, which was the home of Lord Blodrell and his family, and was a small fortress in its own right. Other buildings included the chapel, the barracks, the stables, the refectory, the armoury, and the numerous living quarters for the servants and merchants.

Inside the main gate was a huge courtyard from which radiated the streets, alleyways, and thoroughfares by which the numerous inhabitants found their way around the castle. It was a truly fitting residence for one of the Great Lords of Gothria.

Wildren and Barnabus passed through the huge gates, and Barnabus could see the massive winding mechanism that controlled the enormous portcullis.

Barnabus stopped immediately inside the gate. Castle Blodrell was like a town in its own right, and crowds of people were criss-crossing the courtyard, each intent on errands of their own. Some carried food and some carried weapons, while others were clearly craftsmen, carrying tools or pieces of wood or metal. And there were soldiers. Lots of soldiers. There was much more activity here than there had been in the village.

Barnabus immediately felt at home.

This is just like the streets of Waxminster!

He realised that he'd felt uneasy out in the countryside, and that he was truly a city boy.

He breathed in the dust of the courtyard, and with it the familiar smells of street-life. Cooking, wet laundry, horse droppings, and a liberal dose of sweat.

"I like it here, Wildren," he said. "It feels like home."

"I'm glad," replied Wildren. "Now, let's find Elvarin."

Wildren strode purposefully across the courtyard, and Barnabus followed him eagerly. Now that he felt himself to be in a familiar environment he was able to relax, and his natural curiosity took over. He looked around keenly, and carefully observed all the sights and sounds of the castle.

Wildren led him into the tall entrance of the Keep, the central building of the powerful stronghold. It was built of huge blocks of stone, like everything else in the castle. They entered by the imposing doorway, and went up the wide stone staircase. All around them the walls were decorated with shields and spears, crossed swords and axes. To Barnabus's eyes it was a dream come true. He'd always wanted to see inside a knight's hall, and now, at last, he was doing it! Huge flags hung down from the high ceiling, flags captured in battle. There were flags he'd never seen before, some of them weird and wonderful, but all of them majestic.

The enormous staircase curved upwards, until it reached a wide landing. This branched off into many corridors, and Wildren led Barnabus along one of them. Finally, he stopped outside a pair of wide double doors. He briskly knocked, pushed the doors open and marched through them with Barnabus close behind him.

They were inside a tall, wide room, with windows that reached all the way up to the ceiling. It was an entrance hall to a suite of rooms, with several doors leading to the other rooms within. Wildren knocked on one of them, and opened it without waiting for an answer. Barnabus followed him inside once more. In this room there was a table, with chairs, book-cases, cupboards, and a huge four-poster bed in the corner.

Wildren did not look happy. Barnabus was sure he was going to lose his temper. "Master Elvarin!" he shouted. Barnabus jumped. The untidy pile of blankets on the bed twitched. "Master Elvarin, I expect better than this!" he said sternly, and marched over to the bed. He took hold of the blankets and firmly pulled them away, dropping them onto the floor.

Elvarin lay uncovered on the bed, wearing pink silk pyjamas. He was asleep, and snoring softly. He jerked, woke up, and stretched. "What?" he murmured. "What's happening? I'm cold. Where are my blankets?"

"Master Elvarin, get up! You knew Master Barnabus was coming! For heaven's sake, get out of bed!"

"Oh, Wildren," sad Elvarin, sadly. "I was having such a nice dream!" He turned over onto his side, and curled up once more. Almost immediately, the sound of snoring resumed.

Wildren was furious. "Get out of bed, you lazybones!" he shouted at the top of his voice.

Elvarin's eyes shot open, and he sat up with a jerk. He threw his legs over the side of the bed, and stood to attention. "Yes, Wildren," he stammered. "I'm sorry, Wildren."

"I should hope so!" Wildren was incandescent with rage. Barnabus was astonished to see the old man so angry, and was surprised to feel scared himself. "Now get dressed, you lazy boy! Hurry up!"

"Yes, Wildren," said Elvarin, and he rushed to the dressing room door, which he flung open, and quickly ran through.

Barnabus looked at Wildren. The old man was red in the face with anger. In fact, he didn't seem such an old man at all. Barnabus could well imagine he was really a knight himself. Or, at least, had been, when he was younger.

Wildren took a deep breath, controlled his temper with an obvious effort, and turned to Barnabus. He forced a smile.

"I'm sorry, Barnabus, but Elvarin is not always as, ah, punctual as he should be."

"Don't worry," said Barnabus, bemused by the fuss. "I'm in no hurry." Which was true. He wasn't. He had nowhere to go, and the only thing he was waiting for was to find out why he was there at all.

Then, before he could say anything else, the dressing room door burst open, and Elvarin rushed back into the room, his red hair combed and neat. He was wearing a smart tunic with clean leggings and leather boots.

"I'm ready, Wildren," he said, apologetically. "But do you think there would be time for any breakfast at all?" he pleaded.

"Certainly not, Elvarin. You should have been up hours ago, and you could have had your breakfast then. Now you'll just have to wait for supper."

"Oh. I see. All right, then," said Elvarin. Barnabus was surprised he didn't argue, but he was beginning to suspect that everything here was not quite what it appeared to be. Wildren didn't behave like a servant or a squire at all. In fact, rather surprisingly, he seemed to be in charge.

Maybe they just pretend he's a servant when they're outside.

"So, let us deal with what is important, Elvarin. Which is what I keep trying to tell you. Prioritise!" Wildren was talking to Elvarin like a schoolmaster, and a strict one at that.

"Yes, Wildren," answered Elvarin meekly, like a small child.

"So, let us sit down and discuss the situation with our good friend, Barnabus, who has so kindly travelled all the way from Waxminster to be with us." Barnabus thought this was bending the truth somewhat. He'd been kidnapped and brought here against his will, and Wildren was talking as if he'd travelled there intentionally. Still, it never hurt to be presented in a good light. "And whom you have not yet even greeted, Elvarin!"

Elvarin took the hint. "Barnabus!" he cried, genuinely pleased. "It's so good to see you again!" He took hold of his hand and shook it. "Thank you so much for coming! I can't tell you how much I appreciate it!"

"No problem," he replied. "It's my pleasure!" Sometimes a little lie helped things along too.

Wildren indicated a large table, elaborately carved and beautifully polished, with three exquisite chairs placed around it.

"Master Barnabus if you will sit there" – Wildren indicated one of the chairs – "and Master Elvarin there. I will sit here. Good. Are you properly awake, now, Elvarin?"

Although Wildren spoke respectfully, Barnabus could detect the steely edge of command in his voice.

"I'm fine, thank you, Wildren," Elvarin replied, politely.

"And you, Barnabus?" Wildren asked, kindly.

"Yes, thank you, Wildren." Barnabus felt as though they were playing some kind of game.

"Good," said Wildren. "Now then, let us discuss our reasons for bringing Barnabus here. Are you ready, Elvarin?" Elvarin was doing his best to stifle a yawn. "Master Elvarin?" asked Wildren, with one eyebrow raised.

"What?" replied Elvarin, shaking his head. "Oh, yes, of course I'm ready, Wildren. Just a bit hungry, that's all."

"Good," replied Wildren, crisply. "That will keep you from falling asleep again. Hopefully," he added.

Elvarin said nothing. He was used to Wildren putting him in his place.

"Now, let us get down to business," said Wildren. He turned to Barnabus. "First of all, let me apologise for bringing you here in such an undignified manner. We had no other way to do it, I'm afraid, so I'm sorry for the inconvenience."

There was a silence, and Barnabus realised that he was supposed to say something. "Oh, don't worry," he said. "Spider and Wagsnatch are, well, sort of old friends of mine, you could say."

"A spider and a what?" asked Elvarin, confused.

"They were the two people who, well, who brought me here."

"Quite so, Barnabus. Anyway, here you are and, I hope, in good shape, because, you see, we have a favour to ask of you, don't we, Elvarin?"

"Do we? I mean, we do, don't we, Wildren?"

"Yes, we do, Elvarin, and I'm sure you would like to ask him yourself, wouldn't you?"

"Oh. Yes, indeed, Wildren. Ahem." Elvarin cleared his throat, and turned to face Barnabus. He looked wide awake at last, and was completely serious. "Barnabus," he said, very politely, "I wonder if you would be so kind as to be my bodyguard. I'll pay you well, of course."

Chapter 11

An Unwelcome Visitor

Barnabus was stunned. He hadn't known what to expect, but it certainly wasn't this. "What?" he asked.

Wildren responded. "I know this must come as a bit of a surprise, Barnabus, but we need your help. Tell him, Elvarin."

"Yes, Wildren. You see, Barnabus, you did me a massive favour when you knocked old Gratzenburg off his horse at the tournament. I've been the toast of society ever since then, and my father - who you'll meet shortly - can't buy me enough presents. He never thought his own son would turn out to be such a fine jouster!" Elvarin smiled to himself, as though enjoying his own success. "Unfortunately," he continued, "there have been other consequences as well, haven't there, Wildren? Show him."

Wildren reached under the table, and brought out a roll of parchment with a ribbon around it. He untied it, unrolled it, and handed it to Barnabus. He studied it briefly, and then, in a puzzled voice, said, "What does it say? I can't read."

"Ah, I'm sorry, Barnabus," said Wildren. "Don't worry, we'll remedy that while you're with us. Please, let me." He took the parchment back and read aloud.

"'The Black Knight is obsessed with his defeat at the Waxminster tournament. He can talk of nothing else but having his revenge. He plans to hire an assassin and have Elvarin killed by the autumn full moon.' Which is in three weeks time, as you know. That's the end of the report. At least, all you need to know." He rolled up the parchment again, and put it back under the table.

"How do you know this?" asked Barnabus. "Where did the paper come from?"

Barnabus was perfectly used to secrets and subterfuge, but not being able to read, he'd never thought of using paper to convey messages.

"My father has agents," said Elvarin, proudly. "He has spies all over the country. You don't get to be as rich and powerful as he is without a network of spies to rival the King's. So it was one of his agents in the court at Pendarion who sent this to us."

"But what's it got to do with me?" asked Barnabus, confused.

"It's simple," said Wildren. "Elvarin's father, Lord Blodrell, has doubled and re-doubled the security in the castle, and in Blodrell Sonnet generally. You've seen all the soldiers around the place. He's taken all the steps money can pay for to protect Elvarin. But I feel they may be of little use against a skilled assassin. And rest assured, Sir Gratzenburg will pay for the very best. His pride has been injured, and he will do anything he can to have his revenge."

"Then if Elvarin's father will pay, you must get him the best bodyguard!" protested Barnabus.

"You're right," said Wildren. "And that's what we've done. We've got you!"

"Me?" exclaimed Barnabus, completely surprised.

"Yes, you. You're the best of the best," said Wildren. "You are resourceful. You are imaginative. You are a fighter. But most of all, you are one of the legendary Street Knights of Waxminster, and you never turn down a call for help."

"Well, I suppose that's true," said Barnabus, feeling flattered. "But what can I do that a squad of soldiers can't?"

"You, Barnabus, are to be Elvarin's constant companion. Lord Blodrell can fill the castle with thousands of soldiers, but it is the person of Elvarin that must be protected. You will be the last line of defence. You will accompany Elvarin day and night. You will eat with him, you will sleep near to him, and you will use your considerable skills to protect him from whatever gets through the walls and past the guards."

"But what if I don't want to do this?" asked Barnabus, earnestly. "You know I've got no experience of living the life of a lord! I belong in the streets of a big city, not inside the walls of a castle!"

"If you don't want to stay, then I'll arrange for you to travel home tomorrow. In a comfortable carriage, with a purse full of gold. And no hard feelings." Wildren smiled at Barnabus, which made it even harder to turn him down.

"And if I stay?" asked Barnabus, tentatively.

"If you stay, you do your best to protect Elvarin, and when the threat is over, we'll send you home in a comfortable carriage, with a purse full of gold. Unless you want to stay here, of course."

"So I can go home now, if I want to?"

"Of course."

"And if I stay, I can go home any time I want to?"

"Of course."

"And whenever I go, I'll take some gold with me?"

"Of course."

"Then I'll stay."

Both Wildren and Elvarin gave a sigh of relief. They hadn't realised they'd been holding their breaths.

"Thank you, Barnabus," said Wildren. He held out his hand, and Barnabus took it. "You've no idea how grateful I am."

"Me, too," said Elvarin, taking his other hand and shaking it vigorously. "You're my last hope."

Barnabus was embarrassed. The weight of Elvarin's expectations sat heavily on his shoulders. He wasn't sure he could meet them. He slowly retrieved his hands and cleared his throat.

"Right then," he said. "If I'm to work here, where do I begin?"

"Excellent, Barnabus," said Wildren, rubbing his hands together. "A most business-like attitude. That's what I like. So, let's get to work. Hmm, how about some decent clothes to begin with? I'm sure your present outfit is fine for the streets of Waxminster, but here you will be seen at Lord

Blodrell's table …. and then, something to eat. How does that sound?"

"Excellent," burst in Elvarin. "I'm starving!"

"I have no doubt about that, Elvarin, but I was talking to Barnabus!" said Wildren, dryly. Then he smiled at Barnabus, and said, "Good. Well, I'll have some food sent up while you, Elvarin, find some clothes for Barnabus. On second thoughts, he'd better have a bath first."

And so Barnabus's life in the castle began. If he was to be Elvarin's personal bodyguard, then he had to be his constant companion. He had to eat at his table, sleep in his room, and sit in on his lessons. The only time he had to himself was when Elvarin was having fencing training – which was every morning – and so was surrounded by armed soldiers in the weapons yard.

Travel outside the castle was forbidden to both of them. Elvarin – and therefore Barnabus – had to remain inside it until the threat was over. This could have been claustrophobic for them both if it wasn't for the fact that Castle Blodrell was so big.

One of the first things Elvarin had done with Barnabus - when he was washed, clothed and fed - was to take him on a tour. Castle Blodrell was like a smaller version of Waxminster, and Barnabus quickly recognised the same basic elements of town life. Stables, blacksmiths, granaries, bakeries, butchers, and tradesmen of all sorts were there. The castle was big enough to accommodate all of the population of Blodrell Sonnet in an emergency, and so was kept permanently well stocked, should such an emergency arise.

This meant that it was, in effect, a town in its own right, with all the layers of society that would be expected in one.

Barnabus felt rapidly at home. Because he was seen with Elvarin he was treated with the greatest of respect. Although his position was that of bodyguard, the rest of the castle knew him as Sir Elvarin's squire, a position of authority. They were always seen together, so that Barnabus felt as though he was permanently in the public eye.

This was a strange experience for him. In Waxminster he used all of his skill to remain unseen, to act in secret, to be invisible and untraceable. His places of action were the shadows, the sewers and the rooftops.

Here, he was in the bright light of day all the time. He couldn't be more conspicuous, more visible, or more recognisable. Dressed in the bright, gaudy, red and gold of the Blodrell livery, he was every inch a member of Lord Blodrell's household, and a significant one at that.

This had the advantage that he could explore the castle and its grounds at will. While Elvarin had his morning weapons training, Barnabus had the time to do whatever he wanted. He used it well, patrolling every inch of the castle and the buildings contained within it – the granary, the chapel, the barracks, the market, the storage areas, and so on. He even explored the sewers, a network that was much smaller than the one he was used to in Waxminster.

Within a week he felt as though he'd been there all his life. Of course, some things he would never get used to. Every evening he had to serve Elvarin at the high table. Lord Blodrell was there most of the time – when he wasn't travelling – and he studiously avoided looking at Barnabus as though he was something beneath his notice. Wildren had told Lord Blodrell that Barnabus was a nephew of his from Waxminster who'd been trained as a bodyguard to young lords.

Wildren assured Barnabus that Lord Blodrell approved of the arrangement, even though he didn't show it. Lord Blodrell accepted Wildren's advice on this, as on so many things.

Barnabus soon came to realise that although Wildren was a quiet, unassuming white-haired old man, he was a power to be reckoned with in the castle. He seemed to be Lord Blodrell's representative in all matters practical, political and financial, and every single castle-dweller jumped to attention when Wildren gave them an order.

It took Barnabus a while to realise that some of this respect for Wildren had rubbed off on him, too.

Making use of his new-found authority he found his way into every nook and cranny, every cellar and dungeon, and the garret of the highest tower. In short, Barnabus used every moment of his spare time to improve his knowledge of the castle, so that he knew it like the back of his hand.

His relationship with Elvarin got better, too. Now that Barnabus was dressed smartly, Elvarin seemed to have forgotten that he was a Street

Knight, and he treated him as if he was a member of the nobility, just like himself.

What's more, Wildren insisted on Barnabus being present during Elvarin's schooling in the afternoon. He gave him special lessons to teach him how to read, and soon he was capable of taking part in, and at least partially understanding, Elvarin's lessons.

All was going rather well, and Barnabus had almost forgotten the real purpose of his stay in Castle Blodrell, when one day the afternoon lesson was interrupted by the sound of screaming coming from the courtyard below. Elvarin rushed to the window and looked out.

"Oh no!" he cried, holding his head in his hands. "She's back!"

"Back?" said Barnabus, looking up from the book he was trying to read. "Who's back?"

Wildren replied, "I know. It's Eleanora."

"Eleanora?" asked Barnabus, looking from Wildren to Barnabus and back again.

"Yes," said Elvarin, miserably, "my sister."

Eleanora

Chapter 12

From Bad to Worse

"I didn't know you had a sister!" said Barnabus, curiously.

"I wish I hadn't," replied the gloomy Elvarin.

"Now, now, Master Elvarin," said Wildren, reproachfully. "That's no way to speak about your twin!"

"A twin sister!" exclaimed Barnabus, impressed. He went over to the window too, and looked down into the courtyard below.

A group of horses with their riders had just ridden through the main gate, and the lead rider was shouting at one of the stablehands. His voice sounded like that of a girl screaming in frustration, although he looked, from his clothes, like a young lord.

"Is that a boy or a girl?" asked Barnabus, turning back from the window.

"It's a girl," replied Elvarin, wearily. "It's my dear sister."

"Then why is she dressed like a man?" asked Barnabus, curiously.

"Because she thinks she is one," groaned Elvarin.

Wildren butted in. "The lady Eleanora has always been more interested in the affairs of men than the affairs of women. An attitude which her father has encouraged. She is also not the most patient of people, as you may have noticed."

Barnabus couldn't help but hear the explicit demands the screaming voice was making for the comfort of her and her companions' horses.

"She always gets what she wants," sighed Elvarin, "always."

"Why did you never mention her to me?" asked Barnabus.

"Why?" asked Elvarin. "Because I never, ever think about her, that's why. Not unless she is forcing herself upon me, which is what is about to happen."

There was a knock on the door.

"Come in," called Wildren. The door opened, and a page came in. He bowed, and addressed Elvarin.

"Lord Blodrell requests the pleasure of the company of Sir Elvarin, Master Wildren and Master Barnabus in the Armoury immediately, if you please."

"Thank you, Florant," said Wildren. "We'll come straight away."

The page left, closing the door behind him.

"You see," said Elvarin. "She's bent father's ear already. He must have known she was coming, and not told us. Come on, we'd better go."

"I think you're right, Master Elvarin," said Wildren. "It's not a good idea to keep your father waiting – especially if Eleanora is here!"

"A double dose of terror!" muttered Elvarin, bitterly.

Barnabus followed Wildren and Elvarin as they left the room and made their way to the Armoury. This was one of Lord Blodrell's favourite places, probably because the arrangement of weapons displayed around the walls was designed to intimidate anyone who went there. And also because they reminded him of his own youth, when he fought in the Eastern wars. It was a huge room. Swords, spears, knives, axes, longbows, crossbows and arrows were stacked in frames. Shields, armour and helmets were piled on shelves. Doors led off to more specialised rooms where breastplates, greaves, hauberks, gambesons and entire suits of armour were stored. This was the heart of Lord Blodrell's military power. With the hardware collected in this network of rooms he could equip an army, and sometimes did, especially when the king required it.

When Barnabus arrived with Wildren and Elvarin, Lord Blodrell was pacing up and down, sweeping a huge sword through the air. The activity suited him. Lord Blodrell was built to be a knight. Or, at least, had been. He was a huge man, well over six feet tall, and powerfully built. His stocky frame contained not one ounce of fat – he was made of solid muscle. In his younger days he'd been a champion jouster, but now considered himself too old to go falling off horses onto the hard ground. He had shoulder length hair – like Wildren – but his was bright red. So were his beard and moustache. Despite his age, there were no grey hairs at all.

As they walked into the Armoury, Lord Blodrell handed the sword to Captain Draxa and turned to meet them. Draxa put the sword into a rack and gave them his attention too.

"Wildren. Elvarin. Barnabus," growled Lord Blodrell. He was a man of few words. His face looked as though it had been in many fights, and wore a permanent frown. He was a hardened old warrior.

Barnabus liked him. He always spoke clearly and directly, and was scrupulously fair. It was hard to imagine that this tough old knight was the father of soft and lazy Elvarin.

"Father," said Elvarin, walking up to him, while Wildren and Barnabus held back, and bowed. "We came straight away. Is Ellie here?" He looked around nervously.

"She's changing out of her travelling clothes," Lord Blodrell replied, gruffly. "I received a letter from her yesterday, telling me she was coming. She asked me to arrange a meeting as soon as she arrived. She has news from court, apparently."

"Typical," said Elvarin, wearily. "When she wants a meeting, we jump to attention, and yet she's late for it herself!"

"Thank you, dear brother, for your concern," spoke a female voice. It was coming from another entrance. "And yes, thank you, I had a safe and comfortable journey."

The speaker came through one of the many doors to the Armoury, and Barnabus saw Eleanora close up for the first time. When he'd seen her from the window, she'd been wearing men's travelling clothes. Now, she was dressed in a full-length green gown, which set off her long red hair. She was clearly Elvarin's twin, and looked like a female - and prettier - version of him. She strode across the room, walked right up to Elvarin, and kissed him on the cheek. He pulled a face, as though he'd been stung.

"Nice to see you too, brother," she said, sarcastically. Then she turned to Wildren, and enclosed him in a warm hug. "And you, teacher. It's very good to see you."

"And you, my dear pupil," he replied, returning the embrace.

"Captain Draxa," she said politely, curtseying to the old warrior.

"My lady," he replied, inclining his head slightly.

Then she turned to Lord Blodrell, and knelt before him with her head bowed. "Dear daddy, I'm so happy to see you again," she said, respectfully.

"Come, come, child," he said in his deep voice. Barnabus could hear the emotion in it. "You're not at court now. No need for formality." He reached down with his huge hand, took hold of hers, and pulled her to her feet. She disappeared in his bear-like embrace.

Barnabus could see the bond of affection between father and daughter.

Strange, I've never seen Lord Blodrell treat Elvarin like that.

Elvarin was looking uneasy throughout this encounter, as though he was embarrassed by it.

No, not embarrassed. Jealous.

Lord Blodrell always behaved politely towards his son, but never in the way he was now behaving towards his daughter.

I suppose I'd be jealous too, if I was Elvarin.

Eleanora was still in her father's embrace, and he whispered into her ear. Then, she pulled herself away from him, and her smiling face became serious. She turned towards Barnabus with a scornful expression. "So this is the bodyguard!" she said, condescendingly.

She walked around him, studying his appearance as though he was an unpleasant object. She didn't hide her disdain.

"So this is the one who's supposed to protect my brother from the Black Knight? And how is he meant to do that? Any assassin sent by Sir Gratzenburg will be the best that money can buy. Can we say the same for you, sir?"

Wildren saw that he had to say something in Barnabus's defence, before Lord Blodrell could be swayed against him. "My lady, appearances can be deceptive," he said. "When Elvarin and I were in Waxminster for the spring tournament, my nephew, Barnabus, was – ah, brought to our attention with the very best of references. I am sure that he will prove worthy of our trust."

He can't tell her I'm a Street Knight or she'll despise me even more than she already does. I've got to do something.

Barnabus had been in the castle long enough to know how to imitate an educated accent. He made his voice as deep as he could – no mean feat for a twelve year old – and said, in his best imitation of Elvarin's courtly language, "I trust that my lady will not be disappointed with my services," and he bowed as low as he possibly could.

Eleanora was taken off guard by his extreme politeness. "Yes, well, I trust you will give me no reason to be disappointed," she said, diffidently.

Wildren decided it was time to defuse the situation. "My lady, I must ask you to trust my judgement, as you have done so many times before. Elvarin needs a companion day and night who is capable of defending him. Knights in clanking armour could not fulfil this mission as well as Barnabus, although, of course, they have a role to play. Their job is to guard the castle itself, and indeed, Elvarin's person, from conventional attack. For unconventional attacks I have judged that Barnabus here is eminently suited, so I must beg your ladyship to accept him as one of the family."

Although his words were polite, Barnabus could tell by the steel in his voice that he was not asking Eleanora, he was telling her. Not for the first time, Barnabus wondered who Wildren really was, and how he could exert authority over such rich and important people. Even Lord Blodrell accepted his suggestions without argument, and treated him as an equal.

Despite her fiery temper, Eleanora appeared to accede to his wishes as though they were commands.

"As you say, Wildren," she said, hesitantly, after a short pause. "So shall it be." She turned to Barnabus once more. "I am pleased to make your acquaintance, Barnabus," she said, with ever such a slight curtsey.

Barnabus' mouth dropped wide open. He hadn't expected this. Before he could stammer a reply, Eleanora had turned away from him, and was now facing Elvarin once more.

Barnabus looked at Wildren, who returned his gaze with a hint of a smile, and a raised eyebrow. Barnabus closed his mouth, and raised both of his eyebrows in reply. That was enough to signal the understanding that passed between them.

Barnabus was so grateful to Wildren for bringing him into this world and making everyone accept him – even the fiery Eleanora – that he resolved not to let Wildren down. Ever. Then he turned his attention back to Eleanora, who was addressing Elvarin.

"Now, my dear brother," she was saying, "I'm sure you're dying to know the reason for my premature return. I wasn't due back until the end of the season, but urgent news has forced me to come back earlier." She took a deep breath. "You must know that the court at Pendarion is full of gossip and rumour, but sometimes truth can be found in between the lies. The news there now is more than just gossip. And it's all about Sir Gratzenburg."

"The Black Knight!" whispered Elvarin, nervously.

"Yes, the Black Knight. I still don't know how you managed to unhorse him, and I wouldn't believe it except that so many of those who were there swore that you did. But you must know that Sir Gratzenburg is furious with you! He is openly boasting in Pendarion of his plans for revenge. Of course, he's careful not to say anything in front of the king, for his majesty wouldn't like to offend daddy, yet in all the side-rooms and corners of the court he's boasting of his plan. The news is so bad that I decided to come here with it myself, because I didn't feel I could trust anyone else with it. I've already let you know that he's intent on revenge, and I see you've increased the guard. That's good. However, I've got more news. Bad news."

"What news is so dire it could drag you away from your beloved court, my dear sister?" asked Elvarin, sarcastically.

Lord Blodrell didn't like that. "Elvarin, your sister has ridden a long way to bring you a message, a message which will have implications for your own safety. You will treat her with respect!" His huge, craggy face frowned at Elvarin.

"Yes, father," said the chastised Elvarin. "I'm sorry, Ellie. I didn't mean to make fun of you."

"It doesn't matter," she replied. "You will rule one day, not me, so I suppose you can say whatever you like."

"That's not the point," said Elvarin, "and anyway, I can't help being older than you by three minutes, can I?"

"Enough!" barked Lord Blodrell. "Ellie, continue."

"Yes, daddy," she replied, meekly. "The thing is, Sir Gratzenburg has chosen an assassin at last." She faltered, and seemed reluctant to speak. "You won't believe this. I didn't at first, but it's true. The assassin is none other than Drazagon."

"The Crown Magician himself?" exclaimed Wildren. "Surely not! The king would never allow it!"

"The king doesn't know," replied Eleanora. "And he wouldn't believe it if he did. I've tried to tell him, but he won't hear any ill spoken of his favourite magician. He holds him in too high a respect."

"He always did think too much of that wily old trickster," said Wildren, knowingly. "And I wonder if he isn't a little bit scared of him as well. This is bad news, Ellie, make no mistake, but we thank you for it. On the other hand, with this knowledge we are at least forewarned. Do you know anything else about the timing? The letter you sent us said that the deed must be done by the autumn full moon, which is only two weeks away."

So she sent the message!

"As far as I know," replied Eleanora, "nothing else has changed."

Only two weeks, and a magician to beat! That's not good.

"This is bad news," said Lord Blodrell, "but at least it gives us a chance to prepare. Thank you, my daughter. Will you be returning to Pendarion?"

Just then, Barnabus interrupted. "Wait a minute," he said. "If we're going to be attacked by a magician, shouldn't we find a magician to protect Elvarin? I mean, what can the rest of us do against magic?"

"This is a delicate subject," answered Wildren, "but the fact is that no magician in the land dare stand against Drazagon. Yes, there are magicians, and ones whose services can be bought, but none of them would dare to face him. I'm afraid we're on our own."

Eleanora spoke straight away. "We don't need magic to beat a magician anyway. We've got strength of arms, and that will be enough. That's why I've come home, to give you my full protection, brother, as is my duty."

Elvarin answered graciously. "Thank you, Ellie, I know you like the life at court. And I never was much of a fighter….."

"I know that well enough," she interrupted, "and I still have no idea how you managed to beat the Black Knight in the tournament. I would've refused to believe it if I hadn't been told it was true by so many witnesses."

"I – I expect I was lucky," he replied. He almost looked at Barnabus, but managed to keep his eyes away from him. "Beginner's luck, I suppose you could say."

"It was more than that," she retorted. "I've been told you outwitted him in a masterly way. There were many compliments on your horsemanship too."

Barnabus was trying not to blush, but he was failing miserably. Wildren gave him a knowing smile, and luckily, Eleanora didn't notice.

"You've been hiding your ability so well that you gave the court a real surprise," she continued. "It was a good plan, brother. Let them think nothing of you, and then impress them with your skill. I wish I'd thought of it." She laughed for the first time since her arrival. Barnabus quite liked it, and her face looked completely different.

She's really quite pretty when she's not angry.

"And I wish I'd seen old Gratzenburg fall off his horse. The pompous old fool deserved it!" She laughed again. "He was so bruised, he couldn't sit down for a week!"

This time Lord Blodrell joined in the laughter, as did Captain Draxa and Wildren as well, so Barnabus thought he should too. Elvarin was the only one who didn't join in. "I'm glad you're all so amused," he said, sarcastically, "but it's not your life that's in danger. I wish I'd never gone to that blasted tournament!"

"Never mind, son," growled Lord Blodrell. "I'm proud of you. The whole kingdom thinks that idiot Gratzenburg had it coming to him, and no-one more than me. Never regret doing your best, my boy. What matters now is how we approach the danger facing us in the next two weeks. Wildren? Any ideas?"

"Well, your lordship, I think the steps you have taken so far have been appropriate. However, I suggest you increase the guards on the gate, and double all the watches, both in the castle and in the village. Do not allow anyone into the castle who is not personally known to the guards. Elvarin must be accompanied by at least six knights whenever he leaves this building, and there must be guards on all the bedroom doors at night."

"What good will these steps do against a master magician, Wildren?" demanded Eleanora scornfully. "He's not going to storm the castle, is he?"

"You're right, my lady," replied Wildren, respectfully, "but we would be negligent in our duty if we were not to plan for every eventuality. Drazagon may try to poison Elvarin – or indeed, all of us – so that he doesn't have to 'waste' his precious magical arts. He may be executing a double-bluff, expecting us to plan a defence against a magical attack, while sending a conventional assassin."

"Wildren is right," said Lord Blodrell, firmly. "Let's plan for the kind of attacks we know about. Wildren, can you implement these suggestions of yours?"

"Yes, of course, my lord," said Wildren, respectfully.

"And does anyone else have anything to say?" Lord Blodrell asked, looking around the room at Eleanora, Elvarin, Barnabus and Captain Draxa.

"I'd like to help Wildren and Captain Draxa plan the defence, daddy," said Eleanora. "Please?"

"Of course, my dear. Barnabus, Elvarin, obey Wildren and Draxa as if it was myself who was speaking. Is that understood?"

"Yes, father," said Elvarin, respectfully.

"Yes, my lord," said Barnabus, bowing.

"Good. Then we are agreed. I'm going to the library," said Lord Blodrell. "I want to find out more about magic and magicians. Wildren, I will speak to you later."

"Yes, my lord," Wildren replied.

Lord Blodrell nodded. "Dismissed," he said curtly, and left the Armoury.

"I must go too," said Captain Draxa. "I have to arrange the extra guards. With your permission." He nodded briefly to each of them in turn, and followed Lord Blodrell out.

Eleanora turned to Wildren. "I'm going to change out of these women's clothes," she said, pulling a scornful face. "They're no good for fighting. Where can I find you?"

"We will be in Elvarin's study," said Wildren. "I will send out my orders from there."

"Fine. I'll see you later, then." She smiled at him, and then gave Elvarin a peck on the cheek. "Don't worry, big brother," she said, "your little sister will look after you." She ignored Barnabus, turned on her heel, and left the room.

Elvarin frowned at her as she went though the door. "Blazes," he said to Wildren. "Why wasn't she born before me? She's father's favourite, and a better warrior than I'll ever be. I always feel so stupid when she's around."

"Don't worry, Elvarin," said Wildren. "You are the heir, and will rule as Lord Blodrell one day. She has matured before you, but your time will come. Be patient. All you have to do is survive this threat, and then we'll focus on your education once more."

"Easier said than done," he said, bitterly. "Even you would be a better lord than me, Barnabus. You've had to fight all your life. What have I done? Nothing. I'm just a lazy, no-good ……"

"Now, now, Elvarin, don't put yourself down," comforted Wildren. "Your sister is who she is. You are who you are. You each have your own strengths and weaknesses, and you complement each other very well. Now, don't waste any more energy depressing yourself, or we will have lost before Drazagon casts his first spell. Come, let's get moving."

Wildren set off for the door. Elvarin and Barnabus looked at each other.

"You heard him," said Barnabus.

"Oh, very well, then," said Elvarin, and he followed Wildren.

Barnabus looked around the empty room. He was facing a magician now, not just any ordinary assassin! He would really have something to tell the Street Knights when he got home!

Chapter 13

A Rooftop Encounter

Barnabus was in a hurry. Wildren had agreed to his plan, and now he was putting it into action.

Captain Draxa had arranged for a guard to be in Elvarin's room in his absence, with two more outside the bedroom door. What Barnabus had to do could only be done at night.

He'd changed his colourful court clothes for tight-fitting black ones, just a tunic and leggings. He wore black gloves and boots, and had darkened his face with ash.

This made it extremely hard for him to be seen on the roof at night.

He couldn't explore the many roofs of the castle buildings during the day, as he would almost certainly be seen. Yet it was vitally important that he should know every nook, cranny and rooftop of the whole castle.

Roofs were one of his specialities. In Waxminster the roofways were as vital to the Street Knights as the highways were on the ground to everyone else. Here, in Castle Blodrell, they would be just as important. Now that those protecting Elvarin had some idea of the danger facing them – and were expecting an attack imminently – Barnabus had to complete his knowledge of the castle.

Wildren had agreed, and found him the black clothes he needed.

As for weapons, Barnabus had been making good use of his time in Castle Blodrell. He'd made himself a leather harness, which held the knives he'd "borrowed" from the armoury and the kitchen, so he was now well equipped with light weaponry.

Roof walking in Castle Blodrell was easy. The walls were made of huge blocks of stone, with gaps in between them that fingers and toes could easily fit into. The roofs themselves were either flat or gently sloping, so there were no challenges to his climbing ability other than the lookout tower. This was the tallest building within Castle Blodrell, and a guard was stationed on top of it, day and night. A fire was always kept burning there, in a metal basket, so it could be seen for miles around, especially at night. The tower itself was a tall cylinder, just wide enough to contain a spiral staircase for the lookout to go up and down.

The time was about midnight, and Barnabus was amusing himself by climbing round and round the outside wall of the lookout tower.

He saw no need to climb to the top and surprise the sentry, not least because that would let him know what Barnabus was capable of. This would completely ruin the whole point of climbing secretly by night. Having proven to himself that the tower posed no challenge to his climbing skills, he clambered down again.

He quickly reached the sloping roof of the refectory, and walked down the incline towards the corner where the drainpipe was. The sky was clear, with no clouds visible at all. There was no moon, but the nocturnal landscape was lit by starlight. Barnabus stood still, and breathed in the night air. It was cool and refreshing. He looked down on the roofs below, and on the massive castle walls beyond. Guards were pacing along the parapet, but they were too far away to see him. When he looked downwards, and gave his eyes time to adjust to the even dimmer light below, he could see armed guards in every doorway and at every corner.

"Amazing!" thought Barnabus. "Lord Blodrell has got a whole army hidden down there!"

It made Barnabus feel quite secure, which was a mistake, because then he relaxed.

In that second he heard a rustle of movement behind him, but before he could turn round he felt a massive blow on his back, between his shoulders. The impact knocked him off his feet, and he fell onto the roof tiles with such force that he rolled and rolled towards the edge of the roof. He was unable to stop himself, and he fell over it, feet first.

It happened so quickly that he had no time to think, but his reflexes came to the rescue. Just as he rolled off the roof, his hand reached up and grabbed the gutter. The impact nearly dislocated his shoulder, but he swung his other arm up so that both hands could grip the guttering.

Far below him the silent street beckoned, and he tried not to look down. Instead, he looked upwards, waiting to see who or what would appear to gloat over his predicament.

A face materialised out of the darkness above him, a face blackened like his own. It looked down on him and hissed. "That will teach you, you spy! Tell me who sent you, and I might let you live."

Barnabus was not fooled by the disguise.

"Eleanora?" he asked. "Is that you?"

"Barnabus?" exclaimed the girl, surprised. "What are you doing here?"

"Well, if you'll stand back, I'll climb up and tell you!"

"Oh," she said, taken aback. "Of course. All right, then." Her face disappeared as she pulled back from the edge of the roof.

Barnabus hauled himself up over the gutter, and back onto the roof again. He rubbed his shoulder, which was sore. Eleanora was waiting for him there, dressed in black, with ash colouring her hands and face. Her hair was tied back in a pony tail. She didn't look like a lady of the court at all.

"What are you doing here?" she snapped at him.

"I could ask you the same question," he replied, as calmly as he could, but inside his temper was boiling. This girl had nearly killed him. They sat down side by side on the roof, and Barnabus dangled his feet over the edge. There was silence for a few moments as they both thought about what to say. It was Eleanora who spoke first.

"I thought you were guarding my brother," she said.

"I thought you were asleep in bed," he replied.

"I spoke first," she responded, sharply.

"All right, then," he said. "I can best protect your brother by knowing every corner of the castle. That includes the roofs."

"And who's with him while you're gallivanting around up here?" she snapped.

"Don't you worry. He's well protected," replied Barnabus, curtly. "And what about you? Aren't ladies of the court supposed to behave in a more ladylike way than kicking innocent strangers off the roof?" His voice betrayed the rising anger he was struggling to control.

For the first time, she appeared to soften, as though she'd only just realised what she'd nearly done. "Sorry," she said. "I-I thought you were a spy or an assassin, so I responded instinctively and kicked you in the back. I did mean for you to fall off the roof. I'm sorry I nearly killed you," she added. Barnabus detected a note of regret in her voice. In fact, she seemed almost close to tears. He started to feel sorry for her, and felt he should cheer her up.

After all, I'm still alive. Her instincts were correct, though. I could have been a spy.

"Well, I suppose I'd have done the same if I'd seen you first," he said. "But where did you learn to kick like that? It was a high kick, right between my shoulders! Do they teach you that at court?"

For the first time since he'd met her, she smiled at him. "In Pendarion there's an ambassador from the east, from Giandhar. His name is Shian-Kra. He teaches the fighting skills of his country. Even to women, because in Giandhar the women learn to fight, just like the men."

"Whoever heard of women fighting?" said Barnabus, frowning. He'd forgotten about the girls of the Street Knights. They didn't seem like ladies to him.

"They do it in the East," burst out Ellie, defensively. "So he sees nothing strange about teaching me. And anyway," she added, "I learned how to be a warrior here, before I ever went to court."

"You learned to fight with a sword and shield? Just like a knight?" Barnabus was impressed.

She's not just a pretty face. And it is a pretty face, too.

"Yes, of course. What's so strange about that?"

"Well, women don't usually…."

"Castle Blodrell is not a usual place!"

"You can say that again!" he muttered under his breath.

"As soon as we were old enough to stand, daddy had Elvar and me trained side by side. Everything he did, I did. Not just school lessons, but warcraft, strategy, riding, falconry, everything. It was soon obvious that Elvar had little interest in being a knight, while I loved everything to do with fighting!" Even through the ash on her face, Barnabus could see a kind of glow. "Elvar learned very little, and I learned a lot. I wish it had been me instead of him that clobbered that lout Gratzenburg! He's always leering at me in Pendarion!"

"So you can joust as well?" asked Barnabus, curiously.

"Of course!" she exclaimed loudly. Then she realised how much noise she was making, and lowered her voice to a whisper. "Of course!" she repeated, quietly. "I can do everything a knight can do! Daddy encouraged me to develop my natural interests, and so I'm as good at fighting as any man! And as good at climbing, I may add, which is why I'm up here!" She said the last part especially proudly.

"You're pretty good," said Barnabus, earnestly.

"Pretty good? You mean, I'm *very* good, don't you?" she replied, teasingly.

"Well, yes, you are," he added, grudgingly. "Does your dad know about your climbing skills?"

"Well, no, he doesn't. It's something I started when I was a girl, and I thought he wouldn't like it, so I didn't tell him. But I love it up here. The feeling of freedom is fantastic!"

"I know what you mean. I love it too!"

Then he thought it was time to change the subject. "Look, do you think you could show me how to do those Eastern things, like high kicking? I'd like to learn. It would be very useful back in" – he hesitated – "where I come from, I mean."

"I suppose I could," she said, "but what would you show me in return?"

He thought for a moment.

"Have you ever been inside the sewers?" he asked.

"The what?" she asked, horrified.

"The sewers. You know, underground," he said, pointing downwards.

"I know what the sewers are! And no, of course I haven't been inside them, you horrible boy! What a disgusting idea! Why would I want to do that?"

"Well, it's one of the four ways to cross a town, or a castle, for that matter."

"Four ways? What on earth are you talking about?"

"Well, the first one is obvious, the highways. They're just the ordinary roads that ordinary people use. Although, of course, they're not high at all. That's what the roofways are, and that's where we are now. They are the second way. The third way is the houseways. That's when you go through buildings. You know, in and out of the windows. The last of them is the underways, and that's when we go through the sewers."

"It sounds disgusting to me, but I'll give it a try. It's a deal then. I'll teach you Eastern fighting, and you show me the underways."

"Fine. Put it there, Eleanora," he said, and held out his hand. He would never have dared to be so familiar with her when she was in full court dress and they were inside the castle. But here on the roof, in the middle of the night, dressed for climbing, there was no social barrier between them.

She took his hand. "Fine. That's agreed. But there's one more thing."

"What's that?"

"Just call me Ellie. Eleanora is for the court, not for home."

"Fine," said Barnabus, smiling. "Ellie it is."

He squeezed her hand, and then reluctantly released it. It had felt unexpectedly pleasant to hold. "When shall we start our lessons?" he asked.

"How about tomorrow night?"

"Done. Let's meet up here again, shall we?"

"Fine. But don't mention it to dad, will you? He likes me to be trained for fighting, but I don't think he'd like the idea of me going down into the sewers."

"No, I suppose not," said Barnabus with a smile. He couldn't suppress the image of Ellie in a long dress wading through the filthy water in the underground tunnels. "So, same time tomorrow?"

"Same time tomorrow."

"All right. First you teach me eastern fighting up here, and then I'll show you the secrets of the sewers down there!"

"I can't wait!" she laughed.

"Just don't tell anyone at court!"

"You can be sure of that!"

Chapter 14

Attack from the Sky

Suddenly, something caught Ellie's attention. "What's that?" she said, pointing upwards.

The clear starry sky contained a single dark patch. It was far away, but it was moving rapidly across the stars, obscuring them as it went.

"Can that really be a cloud?" she asked. "It's moving too quickly!"

"It's very high. Maybe it's windy up there," replied Barnabus, dubiously.

Ellie wasn't convinced. "It's coming this way, and it's coming fast," she said.

The strange cloud was moving towards Castle Blodrell in a straight line from the horizon. Barnabus could see that it was round, which was unusual for a cloud. More accurately, it was spherical. It was coming nearer and nearer. Barnabus could see that it was tumbling, and had a strange texture to it. "That's not natural," he said. "It's not a normal cloud. In fact, it's not a cloud at all. It's a ball of something, but I don't know what!"

"Could it be something magical?" said Ellie, urgently. "We've got to find Elvar! Maybe it's to do with Drazagon!"

"You could be right. Let's not take any chances. I know the quickest way there, across the rooftops. Come on!" said Barnabus, urgently.

"Wait!" called Ellie. "I can't let him see me like this! I'll go to my room first, and change!"

"All right. I'll meet you in Elvarin's room. But be quick!" Barnabus ran across the tiled roof, and leaped across a gap caused by a street. He landed lightly on the roof on the other side, and sprinted up its steep slope. At the top was a wall. He climbed it, ran across a flat roof, and scrambled down the incline on the other side. He looked up. The tumbling cloud was getting nearer, and was much larger. Reaching down, he climbed in through the window he'd left open, and landed in a wide corridor. He ran down it and turned a corner. There he surprised the two guards who were dozing in chairs outside Elvarin's chambers.

"Wake up!" called Barnabus. "Danger! Danger! Wake up!" The guards jumped up with a start.

"What is it?" said one.

"What's going on?" said the other.

"I don't know," said Barnabus. "But something bad's about to happen. Be prepared for anything!"

He threw open the door to the suite of rooms, and found two more guards asleep in the outer chamber.

"Wake up! We're being attacked!" cried Barnabus. The startled guards opened their eyes, and Barnabus threw open the door of the bedroom. Another guard was dozing inside, and Elvarin was fast asleep on the bed.

"Wake up!" shouted Barnabus as loudly as he could, giving Elvarin a violent shake.

"Wha … what is it?" murmured Elvarin, waking up from a deep sleep. "Who are you? Guards! Guards!" he cried in panic. It was dark, and Barnabus was still wearing his black clothes and had ash on his face.

"Don't be silly, Elvarin, it's me, Barnabus!" He'd forgotten he'd disguised himself. He grabbed Elvarin's shirt from a nearby chair, and rubbed his face with it. "See? It's me!"

"Oh, you gave me such a fright!" said Elvarin, breathlessly, and he fell back onto the bed. "What's going on?"

Just then, Ellie burst into the room. She'd washed her face to remove the ash, and had thrown a night-dress over her black clothes. She was carrying a long knife.

"Is he all right?" she demanded, running to the bed.

"Yes, so far," said Barnabus. "But I don't know how much time we've got."

He ran to the window, and Ellie joined him there.

"Elvar!" she cried. "Come and look at this!" He jumped out of the bed and ran to the window too. All three of them looked upwards.

The tumbling cloud was now rushing down from the sky towards the castle. It looked like a cluster of living creatures, all weaving in and out of each other.

"It's coming for me!" cried Elvarin.

"Get away from the window!" shouted Barnabus forcefully, grabbing hold of Elvarin.

"We must get out of this room!" screamed Ellie, and the three of them rushed to the door. The guard, now fully awake, followed them as they charged through into the outer chamber, slamming the bedroom door behind them. The two guards who'd been sleeping there were waiting for them.

"Stay here!" said Barnabus, taking command. "It'll strike in a few seconds. Weapons ready!" He drew two knives out of his harness, and handed one to Elvarin.

They stood in silence.

This is what we've been waiting for.

Barnabus put his hand to his chest, and pressed the medallion under his tunic to his skin.

Mother, protect us all.

Barnabus was expecting to hear the sound of the bedroom window being smashed. Instead, all was quiet. Totally silent. He looked at Ellie and Elvarin, and the three guards who stood with them, each waiting nervously for whatever might happen next. Their thoughts were interrupted by a terrible screaming sound coming from somewhere outside of Elvarin's chambers.

Barnabus was the first to pull the door open, and rush out into the corridor. The screaming sound was coming from the floor above.

"Keep your weapons ready!" he yelled, and charged up the stairs.

As he got to the next floor, the screaming stopped. He saw that the door to Lord Blodrell's chambers was open. He ran to it, and dashed inside, followed closely by the others.

The door to Lord Blodrell's bedroom was open, and blood was splattered everywhere.

Barnabus dashed to the door, and looked inside.

The room was full of bats.

They were flying wildly around the room, emitting high-pitched squeaks. The curtains, the furniture, the wallpaper, everything in the room was deeply scratched by their wicked claws. They were particularly gathering in three places – on the bed, and in two separate clusters on the floor.

Lord Blodrell and his guards.

"Daddy!" screamed Ellie, and she launched herself at the bed before Barnabus could stop her. To his amazement, Elvarin did the same, waving his knife wildly in the air. But before they could reach it the bats were on them too, cutting and biting with their fangs and talons. Barnabus didn't wait a second longer. He leaped through the doorway, waving his hands furiously in the air to protect his head.

He needn't have bothered. As soon as he entered the room, the bats swarmed away from him and the whole roomful of them streamed out of the broken window. He ran to it, and watched them disappear into the night sky.

"I'll get you, Drazagon!" he screamed.

He turned away from the window to face the room, and saw the bodies on the floor. He quickly knelt down beside Ellie and Elvarin, both of whom had collapsed onto the carpet, badly scratched.

"Are you all right?" he asked urgently, taking Ellie's hand.

"We are," Ellie replied, fighting back the tears, "but they're not."

Two guards lay dead on the floor, hideously disfigured, and on the bed lay the barely recognisable corpse of Lord Blodrell.

Chapter 15

Elvarin Has an Idea

"There is no doubt in my mind that this was the work of a magician," said Wildren. "Bats do not travel hundreds of miles in a tight-knit ball, smash through a window and kill unsuspecting humans!"

"But I thought Drazagon was contracted to kill Elvar, not daddy!" said Ellie, tearfully. "Why did he attack him?"

They had gathered in the Library the next morning. Wildren was chairing the meeting, which consisted of himself, Barnabus, Captain Draxa, Ellie and Elvarin. The last two were still badly scratched. The deep booming of the chapel bell could be heard, even through the thick stone walls. What was left of Lord Blodrell was lying in state there, inside an ornate coffin.

"There are only two possibilities," said Barnabus, and all heads turned to him. "The first one is that the bats were misdirected, and that they mistook your father for Elvarin. Or, at least, the force directing them made that mistake."

"Yes, that is clear," said Wildren, wearily. The strain of preparing for Lord Blodrell's funeral was taking its toll on him. "And the second possibility?"

"The second possibility is that Lord Blodrell was meant to be killed. That he was the real target after all."

"But why? Why should that be?" asked Elvarin. His eyes were red from crying.

"It's hard to say," said Wildren. "It may be pure evil. Or spitefulness. Or, it may be that Gratzenburg wants Elvarin to suffer before he dies. Or it may be something even more insidious. Eleanora, do you have any ideas? You know the Black Knight better than the rest of us, don't you?"

"Yes, I do," she replied. "And I know how he thinks. When he wants revenge, it must be total. He doesn't just like to beat an enemy. He likes to exterminate them."

"So what does that mean for us?" asked Barnabus.

"I think I know," she replied. "It's like this. Now that father is dead, Elvar inherits the title, the castle, and the land. If **he** dies, it goes, by law, not to me, but to the nearest male relative, who is a cousin of father's. He is none other than Sir Constant Frelling, of Crawheaton. A close friend of - guess who? - Victox Gratzenburg himself." She turned to Elvarin. "So you see, brother, the Black Knight is after more than just old-fashioned revenge. He wants your life, your title, and your property."

"He always was thorough," commented Wildren, drily.

"And greedy," added Captain Draxa.

"But there is a way out of this difficulty," said Wildren, with a mischievous grin on his face.

"And what's that, apart from hiring a magician of our own, which you've ruled out?" asked Barnabus, sarcastically.

"Well," said Wildren, "If Eleanora were to marry, her husband would become the nearest male relative to Elvarin, and he would inherit the title and the property in the case of, ah, disaster befalling the new Lord Blodrell."

"Very funny, Wildren," said Ellie in a sarcastic voice. "Ha, ha, ha. I'm not marrying anyone, thank you very much." She looked at him furiously.

"Then if Elvarin dies, you will have nowhere to live," said Wildren. "Everything will go to your father's cousin, and you will be homeless and penniless."

"Oh," she replied, weakly. "I hadn't thought of that."

"Whereas if you marry while Elvarin is alive, everything will go to your husband if Elvarin dies." Wildren was enjoying his little joke.

"And where do you suppose I find a husband at this moment in time, especially one who I actually like?" Ellie was getting annoyed.

"Well, I was thinking of our good friend, Master Barnabus, actually," said Wildren, casually.

"Me?" asked Barnabus, incredulously. "But I'm only twelve!"

"That's the legal age for marriage, my boy," said Captain Draxa, grinning. "So you are old enough."

"But … but … but …" he sputtered.

"Yes, but no thank you very much," spat Ellie. "That was a very poor joke, Wildren!"

"It wasn't a joke," said Wildren, seriously. "You could do much worse than marry a fine young man like Barnabus. Brave, talented, and handsome too! What more can you ask for?"

"Well, he isn't a nobleman for a start!" retorted Ellie. "The king would never agree to it!"

"Oh, there are many so-called noblemen who cannot equal him in his achievements. Why …."

"All right, Wildren, that's enough of that," said Barnabus. Nobody had consulted him on the subject of marriage, and he didn't like being talked about as though he wasn't there. "Whatever may or may not be solved by marriage, the fact is that we'll soon be under attack once more. The saving of Elvarin's life is our first priority, so I suggest we go through the precautions we're taking to ensure that he survives tonight and the following nights."

"Well spoken, Barnabus," said Wildren, "demonstrating yet again that you would make a perfect husband for Eleanora." She stuck her tongue out at him. If looks could have killed, he would have dropped down dead. "However, I will postpone this topic for now, and agree with Barnabus's suggestion. Let us review the castle's defences. Captain Draxa?"

"Certainly, Wildren. I've been building up our military strength ever since you told me about the danger. The Watch is parading through the streets of the village and the castle day and night. Every soldier is on increased alert. If we were aiming to protect his lordship from a thief, a burglar, or even an army, then I'm confident we'd be successful. However, when it comes to magic, I've really got no idea whether we're doing the right thing or not.

"And there's another problem. I've tried to keep quiet what happened to Lord Blodrell and his guards, but word has got out amongst my lads, and they're scared, I can tell you! And you know what? So am I! Lord Blodrell was in his bed when those bats got him, but his guards were wearing armour, and it gave them no protection at all! Now, my lads don't mind a fight when they've got a reasonable chance of survival, but the bats shredded those two lads, armour and all, bless them!" Captain Draxa paused, and wiped his hand across his forehead. He'd had to speak to the wives of the dead men. It hadn't been easy. "But don't worry, Wildren. We'll do our duty. I just don't know if our duty will be enough to protect his lordship – and the rest of us – from a magical attack. And this seems to be a very black sort of magic, if you don't mind me saying so. I can't help thinking that we need some sort of magic of our own to use against it, if you get my meaning. If I could tell the lads we had something like that, they'd feel a whole lot better, they would. Don't forget, the pressure is going to mount. The autumn full moon is less than two weeks away!"

"Thank you, Captain Draxa," said Wildren. He was visibly moved by the soldier's words. "I will give it some thought."

Ellie butted in. "The Captain's right. We need our own magic to use against Drazagon's magic. We've got courage, wits and armour, but we need something more!"

"I said I will give it some thought, my lady," said Wildren, stiffly. "The point has been made."

He's got something in mind but he doesn't want to say it out loud. Not yet, anyway.

Barnabus trusted Wildren's judgement, so he didn't push him. He knew Wildren would tell him whatever he needed to know when he needed to know it. He anyway had more pressing concerns on his mind at the moment, specifically, what should he do about Eleanora?

To find a girl who could climb buildings and fight was nothing unusual for Barnabus. After all, half of the Street Knights were girls. But to find a girl of the nobility who could do it – that was unheard of! Strangely enough, he felt protective towards her. If she engaged in this fight with the magician, she could get hurt. On the other hand, as a member of the Blodrell family, she was probably a target anyway. Barnabus thought that, on balance, he should accept her as an ally and work together with her as a partner. The soldiers would guard the gates, the walls, the streets and the doorways, while Barnabus and Ellie guarded the rooftops.

Captain Draxa spoke again. "Wildren, what shall we do now with his lordship? We've planned our defences, but what about his lordship himself? Should he wear armour at all times? Should he stay in rooms with no windows? How should he best be protected?"

It took Barnabus a moment to realise who Captain Draxa was talking about. Lord Blodrell was dead, so Elvarin had inherited the title. He was the new lord of Castle Blodrell.

Elvarin himself was still in shock, and his face and hands were covered in cuts. He was in no state to make a sensible contribution to the conversation, but nevertheless he spoke. "What about the cellars?" he asked, shakily. "The cellar under the Keep is vast, and there is only one entrance to it, which is in the kitchen. If that door was locked and heavily guarded, then I would be safe down there. I could have a bed, and food, and be safe until …. until all this has blown over. I think I'd like to try that."

"Come on, Elvar," said Ellie, scornfully, "don't be such a coward!"

"Now, now, Eleanora, Elvarin has a point," said Wildren, firmly. "If he is in the safest place possible, then we can give him the best defence possible. The cellar sounds like just the right location. Captain Draxa, can you make sure that there are plenty of guards? And Ellie, can you help Elvarin to organise his rooms down there? You'll have to take a bed, and….."

"Yes, Wildren," interrupted Ellie, condescendingly, "I know what to do, and I'll make sure that he does it."

"Good. Barnabus, I want a word with you when everyone else has gone."

Wildren spoke with such authority that there was no question that the meeting was over. Ellie, Elvarin and Captain Draxa understood that they'd been dismissed, so they all stood up and left the room without a word. Barnabus stayed seated at the table with Wildren. It was Barnabus who spoke first.

"What is it, Wildren?" he asked. "I really should be helping Elvarin."

"I know," said Wildren, "and it does you credit to feel so responsible for him. That is why I wanted to speak to you."

"Really?" responded Barnabus. "What about?"

"It's like this, Barnabus. Eleanora told me what happened when you entered Lord Blodrell's room."

"What do you mean?"asked Barnabus, puzzled.

"She said the bats wouldn't go near you. That, in fact, they flew away from you and left the room completely when you came in. Why do you think that was?" Wildren scrutinized Barnabus with a cool, calm stare.

Barnabus was mystified. "They flew away from all of us. We chased them away together!" he said.

"Barnabus," asked Wildren, quietly, "do you have any cuts? Any scratches? Did the bats attack you?"

"Well, no, but they were flying away…."

"Ellie and Elvarin are severely cut. Yes, they ran into a room full of bats – as you did – and were attacked by them. You, however, weren't. Can you explain it?" Wildren looked at Barnabus earnestly.

"Well, no, I can't. I hadn't even thought about it, actually." Barnabus was mystified. "The bats just flew away when we ran in. It was nothing to do with me. Can you explain it?"

"I have an idea, although it's not yet an explanation," said Wildren.

"Tell me," asked Barnabus, eagerly.

"Well," said Wildren, "it's like this. I was educated a long time ago. I even went to the University at Raldua, which is what young gentlemen did in those days. I didn't entirely waste my time – like some of them – and was a reasonably adept scholar. One of our subjects was theomancy – magic to you – and I have retained some knowledge of it, although no ability whatsoever. The bats that attacked Lord Blodrell were creatures of magic, there is no doubt. If they avoided you, and flew away because of you, then – you must be a creature of magic, too!"

Barnabus was astonished. "Me? No, no, you must be joking! I don't know anything about magic!"

"I'm sure that's true," said Wildren, nodding wisely. "But you must be a bearer of magic for the bats to have behaved the way they did!"

"What do you mean, a 'bearer of magic?'" asked Barnabus, nervously.

"What I mean is that either you have been blessed by a magician in such a way that your aura has been strengthened, or, that you are carrying an item of magic which gives you protection. There are no other possibilities." Wildren was adamant.

"Well, they're both wrong," began Barnabus, stubbornly, "because ... oh ...." His voice trailed off.

"What is it?" asked Wildren eagerly, leaning towards him.

"It – it can only be my mother's medallion." He reached inside his tunic, and pulled it out. He lifted the leather cord over his head, and took the silver medallion in his hand. "Whenever I'm in danger, it gets warmer, and then I don't feel so scared. I've had it as long as I can remember. Here, look."

He handed it to Wildren, who carefully took hold of the cord. He didn't touch the medallion, but held it up so that he could examine it closely.

"I've never seen anything quite like it," he said. "And the image is so worn and faded. It appears to be a woman's likeness. And the writing on the back is in a language I haven't seen before. This is either from a foreign land, or is very ancient. Where did you get it?"

Wildren handed it back to Barnabus, who lifted the leather cord over his head once more. He tucked the medallion inside his tunic. It felt good to have it back there again, next to his skin.

"They tell me I was wearing it when they found me. It's the only thing I have to remind me of my mother. Or whoever abandoned me."

Wildren understood that this was a sensitive subject for Barnabus.

"Well," he said brightly, trying to be cheerful. "It looks to me as though your medallion has got magical powers. It has clearly given you protection in the one situation where you faced a magical enemy - and probably in many other non-magical ones too, I should think - and I suspect it may be invaluable in our struggle against Drazagon. In fact, it makes you an even more suitable bodyguard for Elvarin."

"I suppose so," said Barnabus, forcing a smile. He didn't like to talk about his medallion. It was too personal. So he stood up and said, "I'd better go with him, then, and get him settled into the cellar."

Wildren nodded. He could see that Barnabus had changed the subject. "Good boy," he said. "I'm going to remain here and study the books, as Lord Blodrell had intended to before he died. It may be there's something here that can help us. Magic is a science as well as an art, and this is a very good library. I will come and see how Elvarin is settling in later on."

"See you, then," said Barnabus, and he stood up to leave.

"And Barnabus?" added Wildren, drily. "Try not to let Ellie kill him before Drazagon does."

Barnabus grinned. He knew Wildren was joking, but he had a point. The twins didn't exactly get on well.

"I'll do my best," he said, and left the library.

Wildren sat still for a moment, quietly thinking. Then he stood up and made his way to the magic section, and began browsing through the books.

Captain Draxa

Chapter 16

Danger from Below

Putting his sadness aside, Barnabus strode across the hallway and skipped down the stairs.

Ellie hasn't wasted any time.

Servants were carrying furniture, food, clothes and bedding to the kitchen, and from there, down to the cellar. Barnabus squeezed between them, and made his way down there, too.

As he descended the cellar steps, he was struck by the smells. As a cool place, the cellar was the principle food store for Lord Blodrell's residence, and each room on the long cellar corridor contained a different item of fruit, vegetable, meat or other foodstuff. As he went past the door of each room, his nose was assailed by the smell of its contents. Ham, sausage and smoked meat, beer, cider and wine, apples, onions and turnips, cheese, bacon and chutneys.

This is making me feel hungry!

Right at the end of the corridor was the room being emptied for Elvarin. Captain Draxa was supervising the constant stream of servants bringing the things Elvarin would need, and taking away big brown sacks.

"What was in here?" asked Barnabus as he arrived, sniffing the air.

"This was the potato store," said Captain Draxa. "And it will be again when the autumn harvest is in. Then it will be full to the ceiling with the winter's supply of potatoes. Luckily for us, it's nearly empty.

We've just removed the last of the old crop, and now we're turning it into a bedroom fit for his lordship." Captain Draxa looked round at the bare brick walls and the stone-flagged floor. Primitive torches of flaming rags wrapped around wooden staves were fixed to the walls, and gave the gloomy underground chamber its only light. "Do you think he'll like it?" he said with a grin.

"Probably not," replied Barnabus, laughing. "It's not exactly what he's used to, is it? Especially the smell!"

"Especially the smell," agreed Captain Draxa, "but it's easy to defend. One door. One corridor. We can pack it with men, and nothing will get through. Does that please you, bodyguard?"

"Yes and no," replied Barnabus, looking closely at the grizzled old warrior. "It'll certainly be hard for anything to get in," he said, "but it will also be hard for anything to get out."

"And what do you mean by that?" asked Captain Draxa, puzzled.

"I mean that if I'm in here with Elvarin and ten of your guards, and something terrible does force it's way in, then we'll all have trouble escaping from it."

"Ah. Yes. I see. An emergency escape route would be good." He looked around the room. There was no way out other than the one they'd come in by. "Maybe we could dig a tunnel ….." began Captain Draxa, but then a voice interrupted him.

"So this is my new bedroom. Very elegant, I must say." It was Elvarin, pushing his way through the stream of servants. "It feels a bit damp in here," he said, scornfully. "Can't we move to somewhere drier? There aren't any windows, either. It's dark and stuffy."

Barnabus was the one who answered. He could see that Captain Draxa was annoyed by Elvarin's attitude. "This room is the easiest to use simply because the potato crop is nearly finished, and the fact that there are no windows makes it much easier to defend. So it's the ideal place, really. And it was your idea," he added, for good measure.

"If you say so," said Elvarin, reluctantly. He looked at the pile of furniture and carpets collecting in the middle of the floor. "I hope someone is coming to tidy all this up. I want to sit down!"

"Are you moving in now, sir?" asked Captain Draxa, barely able to conceal his irritation.

"Well, I thought that was the idea, Captain. We did just have a discussion about my safety, didn't we?"

"Yes, sir. But I was supposing you'd be moving in tonight. The last attack was at night, wasn't it?"

"I'm not sure magic only works at night, Captain. I think I need protecting at all times." Elvarin turned to Barnabus. "Don't you think so, too?"

Barnabus knew that Elvarin was right, however unpleasantly he'd put it. "I'm sorry, Captain," he said. "I know that you and your men are under extreme pressure, but an attack can come at any time...."

Barnabus was interrupted by a booming sound that seemed to come from far away.

"What's that?" asked Elvarin, nervously. "It sounds like thunder!"

"We'd never hear thunder down here, sir," said Captain Draxa. "It sounds to me more like something heavy falling. Here it comes again!"

There was another booming sound, closer this time, and the floor began to tremble.

"I think something's wrong," said Barnabus, urgently. "And I don't think we're in the right place to deal with it. Captain, get the servants out and the soldiers in. Quickly!"

"Yes, Barnabus," he replied. But before he could do anything, an even bigger boom sounded, and the whole room shook. This time the sound definitely came from underneath them, and cracks appeared in the flagstone floor.

"It's below us! They've guessed our plan!" Barnabus took control. "We must get out of here! Elvarin, run for it. You go first!"

Elvarin didn't have to be told twice. He would have run out of the door in a second if he'd been able to reach it. But there were piles of furniture and crowds of servants between him and the only way out. Before he could even move, another huge booming sound came from deep below them. The cracks in the flagstones became much wider, the ground shook violently, and everyone, including Elvarin, was thrown to the floor. One huge crack split the room in half, leaving Elvarin, Barnabus and Captain Draxa on the side furthest from the door.

Before they could recover, a terrible sound came out of the cracks in the ground. It was a rustling, squishing sound, similar to that made when walking through a bog. Before anyone could stand up, there oozed out of the cracks what looked like thick black mud. But it wasn't ordinary mud. It was alive, it was busy, it was seething with activity. It bubbled up out of the crack separating Barnabus, Draxa and Elvarin from the guards, the servants, the furniture, and the way out. The servants picked themselves up and ran away, but the guards remained there, staring at the encroaching mud.

"Get back!" Draxa shouted to the guards, and he pulled Barnabus and Elvarin into the corner of the room behind them. The crack had split the room from wall to wall, so there was no way round it. The mud had quickly spread out from the yawning crack so that it was covering an area far too wide for them to jump over.

Captain Draxa drew his sword, and he stood in front of Elvarin and Barnabus as the mud oozed towards them. As it came closer, they could see that it was swarming with life – worms, centipedes, beetles, and other insects they'd never seen before wriggled, squirmed and crawled all over each other.

"Barnabus!" called Draxa. "What shall we do? Those creatures will eat us alive even before the mud drowns us!"

"Do something!" screamed Elvarin, terrified. "Barnabus, do something!"

"I've got an idea," he said, calmly, "but only one. If this doesn't work you'd better just pray. All we have to do is squeeze closely together."

"What nonsense is this!" screamed Elvarin. "I don't need a hug before I die!"

"Calm down," said Barnabus. The mud was much closer now. They'd backed into the corner, and it was within a few inches of Captain Draxa's boots. "Wildren thinks that my medallion is a magical charm. That's why the bats didn't hurt me, he says. It has a protective power all of its own against magic. If we stand close enough together, it might protect us all."

"You'd better be right," snarled Elvarin, "or we'll all be dead."

"I trust Barnabus," said Captain Draxa, "and my sword is anyway no use against that muck. I'll do it." Captain Draxa sheathed his sword and forced himself in between Barnabus and the wall. He put an arm around his shoulder.

"Oh, all right then," muttered Elvarin, and he squeezed against Barnabus on the other side.

"Hold tight, and hope that Wildren was right," whispered Barnabus, trying to sound more optimistic than he felt.

The mud was rising out of the crack more swiftly now, and had almost reached the door.

"Run for it!" Draxa shouted to the remaining guards. "There's nothing you can do! Just don't close the door! Go! Quickly!" The horrified-looking guards turned and ran, just as the mud reached them.

"Look!" cried Barnabus.

Although it was pouring out of the crack at a high speed, the mud had come to a halt in front of Barnabus. In fact, it had stopped in a clean semicircle, reaching from the wall on one side of them to the wall on the other. It was rising upwards in that shape, as though an invisible curved barrier stood between it and the trio cowering in the corner.

Thank you, mother. I'd be dead without you!

"Master Barnabus!" whispered Captain Draxa, respectfully. "I do believe Wildren was right about that thing of yours!" The mud was rising quickly, as though it was trying to swallow them up as soon as possible.

"By Sersei!" said Elvarin, "You're right! Look at that!" The mud – still packed with wriggling worms and insects – rose higher and higher. The invisible wall held fast, and they could see the multitude of tiny creatures close up. It was not a pleasant sight.

Barnabus, Elvarin and Draxa watched the mud rise even higher, until, having reached a height taller than their heads, it began to curve over above them.

"It's going to get us!" whimpered Elvarin.

"No sir, I don't believe so," said Captain Draxa. "The wall of protection is not just in front of us. It's all around us. It's a sphere of protection. It's around Barnabus, and luckily, around us too. Look!"

It's true! Mother, thank you so much!

Captain Draxa was right. The mud was well above their heads and curving over them in a spherical shape. Of course, as it did so, it obscured the light from the torches in the room, and they were plunged into absolute darkness.

"I don't like this," said Elvarin, squeezing himself even closer to Barnabus.

"I don't think it will last," said Barnabus. "At least, I hope not. Whatever force pushed this muck out of the ground can't keep it up forever. Sooner or later it'll have to fall back down again."

I hope!

"Our air had better last that long," growled Draxa.

Silently, Barnabus agreed with him. It was starting to get stuffy inside their bubble of protection. However calm they might remain, three people still needed a lot of air to breathe.

"Look! What's that?" said Elvarin, pointing. Now that it was completely dark inside the sphere, their eyes were becoming more sensitive. Despite the total blackness, some shapes could be picked out in the seething mud. Spots of luminescence were visible, just enough to outline even bigger worms and centipedes than before.

"Just bugs," muttered Draxa, who was getting annoyed at Elvarin's nervousness.

"No," replied Elvarin. "***That's*** not a bug."

In the faint green glow, another movement could be seen. At first it was just a suggestion of a shape, but then, as it grew nearer, an outline became clear. A green luminous figure became visible. It was taller than a man, with a head resembling that of a lizard. Its long arms had sharp claws at the end of them, and a long tail could be seen glowing through the obscuring mud.

"What on earth is that?" whispered Elvarin.

"I think that is what has been sent to fetch you, Elvarin, dead or alive," said Barnabus. "But probably dead," he added, calmly. He put his hand inside his tunic and took hold of his medallion. It was so hot that it was burning his chest.

"It's a demon!" whispered a horrified Draxa.

The green glow intensified as the creature approached them through the dense mud. Two spots of brilliant pale-green in the creature's lizard-like head marked its eyes, which were looking straight at them. It was hard to see it clearly through the mass of insects swirling in the mud, but its intention was clear enough. It was approaching them with its long, claw-like hands stretched out before it.

Barnabus held his medallion tightly, ignoring the burning pain. He didn't know if their shell would protect them from that monster or not, but he thought he'd try to give it some extra strength. He gave the medallion a squeeze.

Mother, protect us!

As he did so, the foul creature let out a screech that pierced right through the mud. Barnabus squeezed his fingers even tighter, even though his hand was burning.

It's working! Wildren was right!

The creature screeched again. It was deafening.

"What's happening?" yelled Draxa.

"I think I'm hurting it," said Barnabus. "Every time I squeeze my medallion, that thing makes a noise."

"Then hurt it again," pleaded Elvarin. "Drive it away! Please, Barnabus!"

"I'm trying, believe me," muttered Barnabus, and he squeezed his medallion as tightly as he could.

Go! Go back down into the pit you came from! Go and never return!

The creature screeched again, and seemed to shake. Then it took its lizard-like head in its claws and swayed from side to side.

"It's in pain," observed Draxa, hopefully.

"Thank goodness," said Elvarin. "I wish it even more!"

Barnabus was now maintaining his tightest possible squeeze on the medallion, and was willing the creature to go away with all his might.

It appeared to be suffering, and at last it turned around and staggered away, disappearing into the murk. Darkness descended once more, except for the spots of fluorescence in the mud.

"I suppose it's gone back down the crack it came out of," said Draxa.

"I hope so," said Elvarin, "and I hope the mud follows it before we run out of air."

"I think it will," said Barnabus. He had his eyes closed now, and was willing the mud to go down with all the strength he could muster.

"Look!" cried Draxa, pointing upwards. Torchlight had appeared above them. The mud was going down.

"At last!" gasped Elvarin. "Let's hope the ground isn't too slippery when that muck's all gone. I want to jump over that crack and get out of here!"

"Me too!" said Draxa.

"And me," said Barnabus, with a new-found confidence. He was still holding the medallion tightly. It had cooled down considerably. "And then we must have another council of war!"

And now we know we have a magical weapon at last – my mother's medallion!

Chapter 17

A Generous Gift

Wildren had described how the earth tremors had begun while Elvarin, Barnabus and Captain Draxa were in the cellar.

It was as though something had been travelling underground and disturbing the rocks deep in the earth as it travelled, like a mobile earthquake.

The tremors began far away, and their impact above ground could be seen on the trees and buildings which shook as the tremors came nearer and nearer.

"It was that green thing," said Elvarin, as white as a sheet. They were meeting in the Library once more. "It was some kind of subterranean demon, swimming in a sea of underground mud. And it was coming to get me! If Barnabus hadn't been there, I would have been …. I can't bear to think of it!"

It was Ellie who spoke next. "So, it's true then, Barnabus. You have a magic medallion?"

"Yes," he replied. "Wildren was right. He suspected it when he heard that the bats had flown away from me. I was able to use it against the mud demon, although I've got no idea how I did it."

"Nor do any of the rest of us," said Wildren, chairing the meeting, "but we're thankful that you did! For now we must just gratefully accept it – for if that demon had decided to take more of us than just

Elvarin, there is absolutely nothing we could have done to prevent it!"

"So what now?" asked Ellie. "That attack came much more quickly than we'd expected. We thought we'd have at least until nightfall before we were attacked again, but this happened in broad daylight."

"Not quite, my dear," replied Wildren, knowingly. "It's always night underground, so our time of day would have had no meaning for this creature. No, my question is, why was this particular attack made at all? I mean, it was as if Drazagon knew that Elvarin was in the cellar. If he'd sent the bats again, they could easily have been kept away from Elvarin by all the doors he was hidden behind. So how does Drazagon manage to send attacks that suit the circumstances? It's as if he either knows where Elvarin is at all times, or he knows our plans. If it's the first, it's a matter of magic we can do little about. But if it's the second, then one of us must be a spy."

There was a tense silence around the table. No-one spoke, and no-one looked up. It was as if none of them wanted to know the truth. The implications were too awful.

"I refuse to believe that one of us is a traitor," said Barnabus at last. "I'm sure that Drazagon is using his magical arts to locate Elvarin. And if that's true, I've got an idea that will confuse him. I'll give my medallion to Elvarin!!"

"Are you sure?" Elvarin asked, amazed.

"Of course!" said Barnabus. "You're the one who's most in danger, not me!"

"But it's your only real possession," said Wildren, seriously. "Are you quite certain about this?"

"Of course I'm certain! I'm willing to bet that, with my medallion on, Drazagon won't be able to find Elvarin with his magic."

"What do you think he'll do then?" asked Ellie.

It was Captain Draxa who replied. "Well, if I was him, I think I'd have three choices. One is to give up, but if the Black Knight has contracted him there's no way Drazagon can do that. The second is for him to wait until Elvarin takes the medallion off. Then he'll be able to find him again. But that would take time, and neither the Black Knight nor Drazagon are patient men. Remember, the contract must be fulfilled by the autumn full moon, and that's not far away! The third is to employ a spy. If he can make use of a person, an animal, or a demon, to locate Elvarin, then he can launch an attack to suit the situation he's in."

"I think the Captain's right," said Barnabus. "If Elvarin can be kept completely hidden, then Drazagon can't attack him. Of course, there's one other possible outcome of this strategy," he added.

"Which is?" asked Wildren, with one eyebrow raised.

"Well," replied Barnabus, "if Drazagon can't find Elvarin, and can't find a spy who can find him, then he might just come looking for him himself."

"Good idea, Barnabus," said Captain Draxa, banging his fist on the table and making everyone jump. "He peeps his head around the corner, and we chop it off. I like it." He was grinning from ear to ear.

"It may not be so simple," replied Barnabus, "but that's the general idea."

"Hang on," said Elvarin. "Does that mean you'd be using me as bait? I'm not sure I agree with that!"

"You have no choice, my dear brother," said Ellie. "Drazagon's looking for you right now, as we speak. As long as he sends humans or demons after you, we can't hurt him at all. But if he comes for you himself, we stand a chance of hitting him back. Or would you rather be running from demons for the rest of your short life?" She gave Elvarin a sarcastic smile.

"Well, if you put it like that," he replied, sulkily, "I suppose I could give it a try."

"Come on, Elvar," said Ellie. "Barnabus here is putting himself at risk by offering you his life-saving medallion. You could at least show some gratitude!"

Barnabus was trying to suppress a grin. He could see that Elvarin was struggling with his pride. His mouth opened and closed a few times, until finally, he managed to speak. "Barnabus, that is a most uncommonly kind offer to make. I thank you for it, and would be grateful to accept." He held out his hand, and Barnabus took it.

"No problem, Elvarin. And I think we'd better start right away, before Drazagon takes us by surprise again!" Barnabus unbuttoned the top of his tunic, and lifted the leather cord holding the medallion over his head. He held the medallion in his hand for them all to see. This time it was Wildren who spoke.

"This is something very special," he said. "While you were struggling to survive in the cellar – unknown to me at the time, unfortunately – I was doing some research in the library. My own university education gave me some idea of where to look, and I have found some useful books. I haven't had time to read them thoroughly yet, but I have at least discovered a section on ancient lockets and pendants. You see, there was a time when magical knowledge was more widespread than it is today, and the creation of magical artefacts more common.

"It seems to me that Barnabus has inherited a medallion of rare power. I believe it to be extremely old, and it may have qualities which we know nothing of as yet, but at the very least we do know that it protects the wearer, and those close to him, from magical assault.

"I doubt, however, whether it would be able to stop a sword, an arrow, or a spear. Its protective abilities only extend to magical attack, which is, of course something extraordinary.

"I intend to research further into these books to find out more about it, but while I'm doing that, we must straight away put into place another battle plan. Captain Draxa, what do you have to say?

"Well, it all depends on his lordship, really," replied the Captain. "The medallion will hide him from magical detection – we suppose – but how will we protect him from conventional spies?"

"I know!" cried Ellie. "He can stay in my rooms! The suite is big enough for us to have separate bedrooms, and my ladies will be forbidden to enter, so they won't even know he's there!"

"What!" interrupted Elvarin. "You must be joking! There's no way I'm going to hide behind a woman's skirts!"

"Not even to save your life, dear brother?" Ellie smiled sweetly at him. "What would you prefer? To carry on as normal until you're killed, or to live in women's quarters so that you can stay alive?"

"Oh, all right then," he said. "But – but just don't tell anyone." He looked around the table. "And that means all of you!"

"Of course," said Wildren, holding back a smile. Barnabus and Draxa were also struggling to remain serious. "Your secret is safe with us. So, now that's decided, let's act quickly. Barnabus?" he asked, with a raised eyebrow.

"Here, Elvarin, take it," he said, handing over the medallion.

Elvarin accepted it graciously. "Thanks, Barnabus," he said. "I'll look after it for you." He lowered the leather cord over his head.

"I'd recommend you tuck it under your tunic, and keep it next to your skin," said Barnabus. "I don't know why, but it feels like the right thing to do. "

Elvarin did as Barnabus told him. "It feels warm!" he exclaimed.

"Yes, it's like that," said Barnabus. He felt uncomfortable about giving the medallion away, even if it was only for a short time, but he knew he'd get it back when everything was over. He felt naked without it.

"Now," said Wildren to Elvarin, "you go with your sister to her suite. Nobody must see you go there, and nobody must know where you are. Discretion is the name of our game. We'll draw the hunter to us, and then he'll become the hunted. You'd better go quickly."

"Yes, Wildren," said Elvarin, humbly. He looked around the table, and then spoke. "I – I want to thank you all for your help. Without you, I'd be dead. I feel so frustrated that I can't do anything myself, and that I'm dependant on your goodwill, but I want you to know that when this is over, I'll reward you all, as the lord of Castle Blodrell." He looked around the table once more, taking in each one of them individually. Then he nodded to Wildren, and stood up.

"Let's be off," said Ellie, standing up at the same time. She put her arm in his, and they left the Library together.

Wildren, Barnabus and Captain Draxa remained seated at the table.

"That was a noble thing, to give away your medallion," said Draxa to Barnabus. "I'm not sure I could have done it if it was me."

"It doesn't matter," said Barnabus. "It's done now."

"Well said," spoke Wildren. "Your modesty conceals a noble heart. It was a deed well done, and one that will lead to the downfall of the wizard, if I'm not mistaken."

Barnabus nodded. "I hope so," he said.

"So what's the plan now, Wildren?" asked Draxa, eagerly.

"Simple, my old friend," said Wildren. "We watch and we wait. Keep your guards at a high level of alert. Make sure Elvarin's own – empty – room is well guarded, and Ellie's is likewise. Barnabus, you live in Elvarin's suite – keep up the pretence that he's in there, and give the impression that he's too scared to come out. That should fool any spies. Meanwhile, I'll call on the Blodrell Bloodhounds."

"The who?" asked Barnabus, puzzled.

"You remember!" replied Wildren. "You've already met them, in the Snake and Cockerel. They're the ones who had you brought here for me."

"Oh, yes," said Barnabus, uncertainly. It hadn't been the most pleasant of meetings. "But what can they do?"

"Draxa's men can guard and patrol inside the castle, and on the streets of Blodrell Sonnet. The Bloodhounds can cover all the rest. They'll watch the countryside for me, and all the nooks and crannies of the village. Between us, we'll know when Drazagon arrives. And make no bones about it, he will come himself this time, and sooner rather than later. He can't afford to fail three times – his reputation would suffer too much! Anyone care to make any bets on how soon he turns up? The autumn full moon is only ten days away!"

"I'm not betting with you," said Draxa. "I always lose!"

"I don't need to bet with you, Wildren," said Barnabus. "I think you're right!"

Chapter 18

Drazagon Strikes

It was only three days later that Barnabus received a message to go and see Wildren.

"He's here," he said.

"Really?" asked Barnabus. "Are you sure?"

"As sure as I can be. The Bloodhounds have spotted a gypsy caravan in the most remote part of the woods, with no horse! It can only have got there by magical means! An old man is living in it, all by himself."

"How did they find it if it's so well hidden?" asked Barnabus, curiously.

"Because I expected him to try something like this," replied Wildren, knowingly. "I told the Bloodhounds to keep an eye on every corner of the forest, especially those hardest to reach. And they did!"

"So what do we do now?" asked Barnabus. There was only one week left until the autumn full moon, and he was feeling a bit nervous, knowing that a conflict was coming and that he had no medallion to protect him. This was the first danger he'd ever faced without it.

"I'm ready for this," smiled Wildren. "What we're going to do is confuse the enemy. Listen, Barnabus. Drazagon knows that Elvarin is here, somewhere inside the castle, because he can't find him anywhere else. We want to make him show himself and play his hand before he has time to construct a foolproof plan, so we have to confuse and disorientate him. This is what we'll do. I want you to take Elvarin out of Ellie's quarters – dressed in women's clothes, mind you, and be discrete, I don't want him recognised – and take him for a walk around the castle at different times of the day and night. As you walk around, have him take the medallion off – just for a second – and put it back on again, straight away. Have him do this in a different place every time, ideally in places which are far apart. Drazagon will detect him when the medallion is off, and lose him again when he puts it back on. This way, Drazagon will get very confused by detecting little bursts of Elvarin all over the castle, so eventually he'll come here himself to see what's going on. And that's when we'll catch him!"

"And how do you intend to do that?" asked Barnabus, curiously.

"Ah, just wait and see," replied the old man, mysteriously.

So Barnabus went to Ellie's suite immediately, and explained the plan to her. She sent her maids away on fabricated errands, and dressed Elvarin in some of her clothes. Barely able to suppress his amusement at Elvarin's embarrassment, Barnabus took him round the castle, and did as Wildren had suggested.

The second time they did it was during the evening of the same day. The third time was after midnight. Then, they tried to be as unpredictable as possible, walking a different route at a different time every day. Servants within the castle soon got used to Barnabus taking his shy girlfriend for a walk!

Meanwhile, the Blodrell Bloodhounds were reporting regularly to Wildren. The caravan was still in the same place in the woods, and the old man was spending most of his time inside it. He'd been seen pottering around in the forest, apparently looking for herbs. His appearance was reported as being nothing special. He was of medium height, with long white hair and a long white beard, but with no moustache.

"That's Drazagon, all right," said Ellie, when she heard it.

He wore a black velvet cloak which didn't conceal the colourful clothes he had on underneath it – "he always was a bit of a peacock," she added - and he had a fur cap on his head. "It must be cold out there in the forest." She didn't sound one bit sympathetic.

He was hardly the picture of a wizard, let alone a dangerous one.

During this time, Wildren continued to meet late at night with Barnabus, Ellie and Captain Draxa in the Library. After three days of taking Elvarin for a walk, Barnabus was getting bored. "How much longer do I have to do this?" he asked Wildren, wearily.

"Not much longer," he replied, grimly. "Don't forget, Drazagon is under time pressure. He's got four days until the autumn full moon, and Gratzenburg will have his guts for garters if he doesn't fulfil the contract. So he's going to make a move imminently. He's been preparing something, I have no doubt."

"And what will we do then?" asked Barnabus. He was nervous at the prospect of fighting the great wizard so soon.

"Ah, don't worry," replied Wildren, confidently. "You will see when it happens. Trust me."

"We do trust you," said Captain Draxa. "But we'd like to prepare a bit more, you know."

"If we prepare too much, we won't be flexible enough to deal with his attack when it comes. It's sure to be a surprise,"

"Well," grunted the Captain, "I don't know about 'too much.' I wouldn't mind preparing a bit!"

"Me too!" said Ellie. She was fed up of having Elvarin in her chambers.

"All right, all right," said Wildren, giving in at last. "So, tell me, Barnabus. If you were Drazagon, what would be your next step?"

"Well, I'd do something to create chaos in the castle. Something dangerous. In that way, Elvarin would be scared out of hiding, and no-one would notice a stranger creeping into the place to have a look around. It would have to be something pretty big, though, to stir up the whole castle. So what could it be? We'd notice an army long before it got here. We're too far from the river to be flooded, so what about fire? That's probably quite easy for a wizard to call up. I think that's the sort of thing I'd throw at us if I was him."

"I expect you're right, Barnabus. So if he attacks us with fire, what do you think we should do?" asked Wildren.

"Stay calm. Don't run around in panic. Don't move Elvarin. And have plenty of water around. In buckets, I suppose."

"Thank you, Barnabus. Can you take care of that, Captain Draxa?"

"Of course, Wildren. I'll do it immediately," he replied.

"Wait! I didn't mean to tell you what to do, Wildren!" said Barnabus, confused.

"Not at all, my dear boy. I value your practical suggestions. If you can think of any more, do let me know."

"Yes, Wildren. Well, if that's all, I think I'd better go back on patrol now."

"And I'd better see how my lazy brother's doing," said Ellie.

"Yes, I must check the guards, too," said Captain Draxa.

"Thank you all for coming," said Wildren. "Same time tomorrow?"

There was no need to reply. When Wildren made a request it was, in fact, an order.

Once out of the library, the three of them went in different directions to fulfil their different duties.

Barnabus was glad of his new-found freedom. He was no longer acting as Elvarin's bodyguard, because his presence in Ellie's rooms would only give away the fact that Elvarin was there. As far as the castle was concerned, Elvarin was still grieving for his father, and so had withdrawn into his own rooms indefinitely. Barnabus still lived there, and kept up the pretence of Elvarin's presence. Of course, this left him quite free, so he spent his time patrolling the castle, especially on the rooftops at night.

He'd never managed to meet up again with Ellie after their first encounter on the roof, so he still remained ignorant of Eastern fighting techniques. She didn't seem to want to leave Elvarin alone at night, even though he was wearing Barnabus's medallion.

He saw little of Wildren, except for their daily meetings. He supposed that was because he was doing all the administrative work of the castle now, especially since the death of Lord Blodrell and Elvarin's withdrawal from public life. He'd had to organise Lord Blodrell's funeral, which had taken place without a hitch. Elvarin had been there – in disguise, of course – although the rumour had been put about that Lord Blodrell's heir was too upset to attend.

Whether or not Wildren had done any more research into magic, Barnabus didn't know. If he had, he was keeping it to himself.

Barnabus ran up the stairs to his own room, within the suite of Elvarin's rooms. He changed into his black clothes, rubbed ash into his face, and slipped out of the window. He easily climbed up the wall until he came to the sloping tiled roof. He swung himself up over the gutter and crouched on the roof top, gazing down at the view below him.

Then he looked up at the broad, starry sky. It felt good to be so near to it.

It seemed so long since he'd travelled the roofways of Waxminster. He wondered how his old team were doing. Izzie would have made Beric the captain of Wickward in his place as soon as he'd disappeared. Izzie! He hadn't even thought of her for…. he couldn't remember how long.

It would be good to be back there. But it was good to be here, too. He had regular food, a proper bed, clothes – and friends. Lots of them. Everyone was nice to him. No-one tried to rob him. Life was easy here, almost too easy.

"Boo!"

Barnabus jumped up into the air and almost fell off the roof. Keeping a tight hold on his temper, he turned round to see who was behind him. It could only be one person.

"Ellie!" he said, in a furious hiss.

She was crouching behind him, dressed in her own black leggings and tunic, with her hand over her mouth. She was shaking with silent laughter.

"Don't do that! You nearly killed me!" Barnabus was close to hitting her.

"Then you shouldn't have been daydreaming!" she managed to say, in between giggles.

"I was not daydreaming!" retorted Barnabus, indignantly. "I was …. I was …." He smiled. "Well, yes, I suppose I was daydreaming actually." He began to laugh as well. The two of them crouched side by side on the edge of the roof, laughing. It was the most relaxed that Barnabus had felt for a long time.

"I thought you were guarding Elvarin," he said. "I haven't seen you up here for ages."

"I can't bear being cooped up all the time," she replied. "And anyway, he's got your medallion. I just had to get away for a few minutes, and this was the best place to come."

"You know…" he began to say, when Ellie interrupted him.

"Look!" she cried, pointing over the castle wall, into the woods beyond. "What's that?"

Barnabus looked in the direction she was pointing. In the forest there was a glow, as if a fire was burning.

"The village is on fire!" cried Ellie. "We've got to tell Captain Draxa!"

"No," responded Barnabus, sharply. "The village is on the other side of the castle. That's the forest – where Drazagon is camping!"

Barnabus had a strange feeling of relief. He'd been expecting some kind of attack, and was glad it was beginning at last. Any assault, however dangerous, was better than the seemingly endless waiting of the last few days.

"What can we do?" asked Ellie, urgently.

"Nothing, yet. He's preparing something. We can't act until we know what it is."

The light in the forest began to flicker, and increased in intensity. It became brighter and brighter, and then – whoosh!! There was an explosion! It was soundless, but could be seen clearly enough. Out of it shot a fireball, which flew straight upwards into the sky. Up and up it went, watched closely by Barnabus and Eleanora. It reached a high point at about cloud level, and then began to curve down towards the castle.

"It's coming here," said Barnabus, keenly.

"It *is* the next attack!" whispered Ellie. She grabbed Barnabus's hand, and gripped it tightly. He squeezed hers in return. "Just when I've left him alone!"

"Don't be scared," he said. "We've been attacked before."

"I know," she hissed. "But each time it gets worse. This could be horrible!"

"Well, I'd rather face a demon up here in the fresh air than down in that dark cellar, like last time!" He sounded more confident than he felt.

The fireball's curving flight was bringing it closer to the castle. "Here it comes," said Barnabus, and he squeezed Ellie's hand even tighter. She didn't seem to mind. In fact, he could feel that she was shaking.

As it descended, the fireball gained speed. They could hear a rushing sound as it plummeted out of the sky, straight down towards the castle.

"It's going to hit!" screamed Ellie, and it did. Right in the middle of the main courtyard.

There was an explosion, and then a flash, as something burst out of the flames. It flew across the courtyard, and into the stables. It flew out of the stables, leaving them burning behind it, and into the chapel. Flames burst out of the chapel windows, shattering the stained glass into tiny pieces.

"It's a fire demon!" screamed Ellie. "Look! It's setting the whole place alight!"

Barnabus could see that she was right. Whatever it was that was racing from building to building at high speed had a roughly human shape, but it was a human shape made out of fire.

"I bet it's looking for Elvarin!" said Barnabus, putting two and two together. "We fooled Drazagon by making it seem that Elvarin was in lots of different places, so he's sent something that can run all over the castle in no time at all!"

"What shall we do?" cried Ellie.

"You and I can't save the whole castle. We've got to trust the servants and the guards to put out the fires. It's our job to protect Elvarin! Come on, let's go!"

He leapt to the edge of the roof. Grabbing the gutter, he swung down through his bedroom window, and was back inside his room again. Ellie followed him.

"This way!" he cried, and ran through Elvarin's suite of rooms to reach the corridor outside, with Ellie right behind him.

Sounds of screaming and shouting could be heard through the windows, and flames could be seen licking at the castle buildings below.

"It's moving fast!" said Ellie, breathlessly.

"Yes, and I bet it'll come this way soon!"

They ran up the flight of stairs leading towards Ellie's suite. On the next floor they sprinted towards her rooms, and were nearly there when a burst of human-shaped flame ran past them, coming from behind. Ellie screamed as it overtook her, burning her arm and her shoulder as it ran past. It didn't go near enough to Barnabus to hurt him, so he could focus all of his energy into running after the fire creature. He was fuelled with anger – anger that the demon was destroying this beautiful place he'd come to call home.

He had a fraction of a second to observe it before it disappeared into Ellie's suite of rooms, leaving a trail of fiery footprints burned into the carpet.

It was of human shape, but appeared to be wearing layers of flame. It was as if a person, draped in veils of flowing silk, had been set on fire. Except that this creature's hands, face, hair and clothes were all *made* of fire.

It's like the mud demon!

That, too, had a broadly human shape, with something evil added to it. This fire demon was similar. It had a head, arms and legs like a human, but everything was made of flame. What Barnabus could glimpse of its face as it streaked past him, though, wasn't human at all. The creature wore a grin of pure evil.

The demon had crashed through the door to Ellie's suite, leaving it in flaming splinters. Barnabus ran in after it, disregarding his own safety, but Ellie held back, scared of the flames.

"Help my brother, Barnabus!" she cried.

Barnabus had no time to answer. The demon had already run in and out of three of the inner rooms. Barnabus could tell because their shattered doors were on fire.

The demon was emerging from the fourth room, and was about to enter Elvarin's bedroom.

"Stop!" screamed Barnabus, but the demon took no notice. Faster than a thought, it burst through the door into Elvarin's room, and fire poured out of the broken doorway.

The heat drove Barnabus back. It was an inferno inside the room. He was filled with frustration and rage. He was supposed to be Elvarin's bodyguard, but he couldn't get anywhere near him!

I can't just stand here doing nothing!

He pulled a cloth off the table, and wrapped it around his head, face and shoulders, leaving a tiny space for his eyes to see through. He dashed through the doorway and saw the demon standing by the massive four-poster bed. Jets of flame were coming out of its hands, directed at Elvarin, cowering on the bed. He appeared to be surrounded by a sphere of clear air, and was unhurt! The fire was bouncing off whatever it was that was protecting him!

The medallion! It works!

He was relieved to see that Elvarin was safe, although he didn't know for how long. At least this gave him a few seconds to take stock of the room.

The flames the demon was directing at Elvarin were bouncing off the protective shell, and hitting the room's walls and furniture, setting it all alight.

Elvarin may be safe - for now - but the rest of the room wouldn't last long.

Barnabus made the hardest decision of his life. He decided it so quickly that he didn't have time to consider whether it was a brave thing to do or not. He unwrapped the tablecloth from around his head and shoulders, and held it out in front of himself, gripping the top corners with his arms outspread. Then, with a scream, he leaped on top of the demon.

"Heyaa!" he cried as he threw the tablecloth over the creature, and followed it with his own weight. He fully expected to be burned to death in an instant, but instead he hit the floor with a crash. There was nothing underneath the tablecloth.

The demon had gone. It had been as insubstantial as fire itself. And with its disappearance, the other flames in the room vanished as well.

"Barnabus!" cried Ellie, running into the room. He was lying on the floor, on top of the tablecloth, with his arms still outstretched. "It's gone! You did it! You've driven it away!" She knelt down to look at his face. "Are you all right?" she asked, in a worried voice.

"What about me?" whimpered a voice from the bed. "That thing was trying to kill me! I was nearly cooked alive!"

"You're all right," said Ellie, scornfully. "You had a magic medallion to protect you. Barnabus only had a tablecloth!"

Chapter 19

The Tables Turned

"I'm not sure that's quite correct, Eleanora," said Wildren, as they sat around the table in the Library, later that same night. "I suspect that Barnabus had more than just a tablecloth to protect him."

The five of them – including Elvarin, no longer in women's clothes – sat together once more in a council of war.

"What do you mean?" asked Captain Draxa. His beard had been singed and his clothes slightly burned by the fires he'd put out. His men were still walking around the castle with buckets of water, determined to extinguish even the smallest remaining spark. Luckily, because of Barnabus' suggestion of the previous day, plenty of containers full of water had been stacked around the castle. Without them, the damage would have been much worse.

"I mean that a tablecloth would certainly be sufficient to extinguish a small fire, but totally inadequate to suppress a fire demon," said Wildren.

"I saw it myself," insisted Ellie. "And my cowardly brother would have seen it too if he hadn't been hiding under the bedclothes." She gave Elvarin a scornful look.

"I was not hiding," insisted Elvarin, "I was protecting myself. That thing was trying to kill me, you know! You were safe! It wasn't after you!"

"Stop bickering, you two!" said Wildren, sharply. "It was Barnabus who took the decisive action. *That* is what we are here to consider, not to apportion blame! Barnabus did indeed extinguish the fire demon, but not only with the tablecloth. He also did it with his own body. Now, I think a fire demon has enough power to incinerate the average human, but this particular human managed to extinguish the fire demon instead. That means he's not an average human at all!"

"What are you getting at, Wildren?" asked Captain Draxa, impatiently. "I've got repair work to do, you know. It's obvious that Barnabus is a cut above the rest, so what else are you getting at?"

"I think I know," said Ellie. "Wildren is saying that Barnabus shouldn't have been able to put out the fire demon. But we know that he did – so why? There must be something special about Barnabus. What is it, Wildren?"

"Good girl. You're on the right track," he replied. "But first of all, I must ask Barnabus some questions. It's that medallion of yours, my boy. How long did you say you'd had it?" He looked at Barnabus intently.

Barnabus felt uneasy at being stared at. He looked at the others, and realised they were looking at him too. He felt uncomfortable at being the centre of attention.

"I've told you before," he said, wearily. "I've had it since I was a baby. They say I was wearing it when I was found."

"And have you worn it continuously ever since then?" asked Wildren.

"Yes, of course," Barnabus replied. "It's my only link to my mother."

"So you've never taken it off until you lent it to Elvarin?" asked Wildren once more.

"Well, only to change the cord, when it wore out. That's all." He shrugged. "There's nothing special in that."

"Barnabus," said Wildren. "It is obvious to us all that your medallion has magic power. What also is obvious to me is that some of it has rubbed off on you. You have a magical protection all of your own, and that's why you were able to extinguish the fire demon. It was your own personal magic that put it out, not the tablecloth."

Barnabus didn't know what to say. What Wildren had said made sense. He'd never taken the medallion off in his whole life - unless he'd absolutely had to - so it was possible that he'd absorbed some of its magic.

"I suppose that could be true, Wildren," he said, thoughtfully. "I've never come across magic before, so I've no way of telling."

Wildren spoke again. "Would you say you've been lucky in your life, Barnabus?"

He was about to reply with a resounding 'no'. He'd been born into poverty and lived his whole life on the streets of Waxminster, struggling to survive. On the other hand, there had been many near-misses in his life. He'd almost been run over by horses or carriages several times, but at the last minute he'd always avoided being trampled. He'd never broken a limb, or been badly cut. Some of the other Street Knights were terribly scarred, but not him. He'd always had enough to eat, somewhere to sleep, and he was the youngest Captain the Street Knights had ever known.

"Well, I suppose you could say I've been lucky in my life, yes," he replied.

"Including jousting, I suppose," said Elvarin, ruefully.

"That wasn't luck, that was skill!" retorted Barnabus, proudly.

"Never mind, boys," said Wildren, hastily. Neither Ellie nor Captain Draxa knew the truth about Barnabus taking Elvarin's place in the tournament at Waxminster, and this was not the time for them to find out. "Whether you want to call it luck or skill, the fact is that Barnabus has had an inordinate number of good opportunities in his life, and he's made good use of them too, no doubt. That's not the question we're considering here. The point I'm trying to make is that he has a certain magical power of his own – of that there is no question. Presumably it comes from the medallion, but – who knows? – he may have it for another reason. But anyway, my point is this. When Barnabus wears the medallion, then the medallion magic combined with his own magic must make him really quite powerful. Possibly even extremely powerful! Remember, he has survived three attacks by demonic forces – those of the bats, the mud, and the fire. So, if ever we needed a secret weapon against a magician, well, we've got one! Barnabus Mudpatch himself!"

"What do you mean, secret weapon?" asked Elvarin. "Do you have a plan?"

"Look," said Wildren, "we've been attacked by the wizard three times. Lord Blodrell is dead, and the castle is badly damaged. We know another attack is coming, because Drazagon only has three days left to fulfil his contract. I propose we don't just sit here waiting for him to attack us once more. I propose we go and hunt him, making use of our own magical secret weapon – Barnabus!"

Barnabus' eyes opened wide. "You mean, we go and attack the wizard, with me as one of the attackers?"

"That's exactly what I mean," said Wildren, smiling. "You have shown yourself to be brave, resourceful, imaginative, and, above all, magically protected."

"Oh," said Barnabus. *We've been on the receiving end for long enough. It's time to hit back.* "All right, then," he said.

"I was hoping you'd agree," said Wildren. "Now, I do have a plan. Listen carefully."

Drazagon

Chapter 20

Facing the Wizard

Barnabus crept through the undergrowth. It hadn't taken long to prepare the plan. Wildren had sent a message to the Blodrell Bloodhounds, and they'd met Barnabus at dawn the next day outside the castle gates.

There were six of them, all experienced woodsmen. Barnabus had asked to take some of Captain Draxa's guards with him, but Wildren had refused. He didn't think they would be able to creep up on Drazagon's camp quietly enough, and Captain Draxa agreed, to Barnabus's surprise. Poachers, deer-hunters, badger-trappers, these were the men Barnabus needed, not armour-clad soldiers. Men who could move silently through the woods and defend themselves with light weapons, such as a bow and arrow, a knife or a spear.

The Blodrell Bloodhounds were there to get Barnabus to Drazagon's camp, and protect him from conventional dangers. The attack was meant to look like an attempt to burn down Drazagon's caravan, in retaliation to the attack of the fire demon on Castle Blodrell. Only Barnabus knew what the real purpose of the mission was.

As for timing, dawn seemed like the right moment. Usually dark magical deeds were associated with the night, and also, Drazagon may not have been expecting a reprisal quite so soon.

Everything had seemed so clear and simple when they were discussing the plan together in the

Library. Now that he was approaching the clearing where Drazagon's caravan was to be found, Barnabus wasn't feeling so confident.

"How did it get here?" whispered Loral, nodding towards the caravan. He was one of the chattier Bloodhounds. "There's no horse to pull it."

"Aye," replied Fandril. "And no path to pull it on even if there was."

"He's a magicker, ain't he, you eejits," whispered Edrix, furiously. "And he can probably hear you nattering, so shut up!"

"Edrix is right," whispered Barnabus, as quietly as he could. "But he probably knows we're here anyway, so we'd better move quickly. Get the torches ready."

Each man had a wooden stave wrapped with pitch-soaked rags hanging from his belt. They gathered together in a circle, creating a shield from the wind, while Barnabus produced a spark with the flint in his tinder-box. It quickly caught the tinder, and a flame blazed briefly. It was enough to light the rags. Six torches touched together in the flame, and ignited simultaneously.

"Now!" whispered Barnabus. "We set fire to the caravan and run!"

They crept out of the undergrowth and sprinted for the caravan, aiming to surround it so they could ignite it from all sides.

Then everything seemed to happen at once. The urgent run suddenly came to a halt as the six Bloodhounds froze like statues, in the act of reaching for the caravan with their torches. Barnabus was the only one who could still move.

"Edrix! Loral! Come on! What's wrong?" he whispered urgently.

A loud voice interrupted him. "They're stuck, boy, stuck. As you should be too!"

Barnabus whirled around, and saw an old man sitting on a log. He wore a long black cloak over colourful clothes, and on his head was a fur hat. He had long white hair and a white beard. His eyes, though, were as black as black can be.

"You! You did it! Let my friends go, or I'll kill you!" Barnabus drew a long knife from his belt and pointed it at the old man.

"Calm down, boy," said the old man, looking not at all worried. "You interest me. You're still moving." The old man smiled a wicked smile at him. "Are you a magicker too?"

"I'm more than that! I'm your death!" Barnabus hurled his knife at Drazagon, but before it could reach him, it stopped in mid-air, and remained there, unmoving.

"Not with that knife you're not," sneered Drazagon. "Now, why don't you come and sit down beside me, and we'll have a little chat. I haven't met anyone like you for a long time."

Barnabus was confused. This man didn't look so evil, and sounded genuinely curious. He decided to make a bargain. He looked around at his friends. They were still as stiff as statues and holding their flaming torches, which would soon start to burn their fingers.

Barnabus turned back to the old magician. "Release my friends and I'll talk to you," he demanded.

"You bargain cheaply, boy. It's done. But they must keep their distance." Drazagon waved his hand, and the six Bloodhounds flew through the air, crashing noisily into the forest. Their torches fell harmlessly to the earth.

"They can stay there while we have a little chat. You are a most interesting boy. Come and sit down here and talk to me. Oh, you can have your knife back, too."

The wizard patted the log beside him. Wildren's plan relied on Barnabus talking to Drazagon, but he hadn't expected it to happen quite so soon. He would have to think fast. However powerful his medallion was, Drazagon was surely more powerful. He plucked his knife from the air, put it back into his belt, and sat down beside the wizard. Barnabus had never seen anyone quite like him before. His eyes were a deep and piercing black, under bushy, white eyebrows. He had no moustache, but a long white beard which sprang out of his chin and grew down to his waist. His nose was long and thin, and his wide mouth was full of sharp teeth, filed to a point. There was nothing in his face to suggest that Barnabus could trust him.

"There," he said, in an old cracked voice, "that's nice. Now we can have a friendly little chat. You look like a fine young boy. Do I know you from somewhere? I have a feeling I've met you before." The old wizard looked intrigued.

Barnabus wasn't sure what to say. It was possible that the wizard recognised him in some way from his conflict with the demons, but Barnabus reckoned it was simpler and probably safer to admit to nothing.

"I've never met you before, no," he said. "You're the wizard Drazagon, aren't you?"

"Indeed I am, my boy, indeed I am, at your service." He smiled a mocking smile, and made a small bow. "I'm glad my fame has spread this far. But, you know, I really have a feeling I know you." The old wizard looked at him closely. "Have you ever been in Pendarion?"

"No sir, I haven't," said Barnabus, feeling as though he was sitting on a park bench, chatting with a pleasant old man. This wasn't how he'd imagined his confrontation with the wizard would be. He was almost having difficulty remembering that this was the evil wizard who had killed Lord Blodrell, and almost killed Elvarin twice.

"Then – I have met someone very much like you. Oh yes, indeed I have. Yours is a very distinctive aura, my boy, an aura so distinctive that I should have known you straight away."

"What?" asked Barnabus, confused. He'd never expected the conversation to take this turn. Neither had Wildren, with whom he'd prepared everything. "What do you mean?"

"I expect you're an orphan, aren't you?" said the old man, with a hint of sympathy in his otherwise cold voice.

"How could you know that?" asked Barnabus, cautiously. It might have been a guess. There were plenty of orphans in the world.

"She never was able to stay in one place, you know," said the old man.

"What do you mean?" asked Barnabus, now really confused. "Who are you talking about?"

"Your mother. She could never have brought you up. I expect she left you at someone's door, didn't she?" The old man looked wistful.

Barnabus was stunned. Drazagon had given him such a shock that, for a moment, he completely forgot about his mission. It seemed as though this dangerous old wizard knew something about the woman who'd abandoned him, and he could think of nothing else.

"Did you know my mother? Can you tell me about her?" His voice was that of a little boy.

"Yes and yes. Of course I knew her! Sersei was her name, and she was the greatest enchantress in the Gothrik kingdom! Money, land, power, were all hers for the taking. But she could never settle down." He let out a deep sigh. "I can feel her aura about you. That's why you were unaffected by my magic, you lucky boy! Which is just as well," he added in a matter of fact voice, "because I would certainly have killed you by now had you not been protected."

"You must tell me about her! Please?" begged Barnabus. "I've never met anyone who knew her! I don't know anything about her at all! Please, tell me something!"

The wizard looked at Barnabus through half-closed eyes. To Barnabus, his face was hard to read, although he thought he saw a hint of kindness in it.

They looked at each other in silence. After a moment, the wizard let out another sigh. He'd made a decision.

"Very well. You asked for it. Sersei is the greatest enchantress the world has ever known. Ageless, timeless, eternal. From time to time she falls in love, sometimes with a mortal, sometimes with another magicker. About thirteen years ago she fell in love again. It was the talk of the kingdom. Then she became pregnant and had a child. Then she, and the child, disappeared."

"What? You mean she vanished?"

"Yes, she does that from time to time, especially when it looks as though she might get tied down. We never knew whether she took the baby with her or not. How old did you say you were?" He looked closely at Barnabus.

"I didn't. They called the day I was found my birthday. By that reckoning I am twelve."

"The right age," said the wizard, nodding. "The right eyes," he said, examining Barnabus' face closely. "And the right aura. You have a good protection, my boy. As good as mine, if not better. Only Sersei could give protection like that. You're a lucky boy." Drazagon nodded to himself.

"No, I'm not," said Barnabus, sadly. "I've got no mother." Then a thought occurred to him. "Then you must know who my father is too! Do you?" He became very agitated.

"Your father? Well, Sersei did like to keep her secrets ...."

"But you said it was the talk of the kingdom when she fell in love and had me! You must know who my father is!"

"Some things are better left unknown, my boy," said Drazagon, firmly.

"But I must know! You must tell me!"

"Do not presume to give me orders!" boomed Drazagon, his eyes suddenly blazing with anger. "I've told you enough! Be content that I've let you live. Do not ask any more of me! My patience wears thin, boy. You and your friends may go now, but I warn you, if you or anyone else returns here, you will certainly die. This I promise, as the Crown Wizard of Gothria!" The sun seemed to disappear behind a cloud, and the world darkened for a moment. Then the wizard calmed down, and the sun came out again. "That I let you live at all is entirely due to my – respect – for the enchantress. That is all. Now, you may go." The wizard stood up and walked towards the caravan. He had terminated the interview.

Barnabus remained sitting on the log with his head in his hands. His world had suddenly turned upside-down, and he couldn't put it the right way up again. The wizard had told him to leave, but he felt paralysed. He had to find his centre again.

Why am I here? he asked himself. Then he provided the answer. *I'm here to help Elvarin!*

Suddenly his mind cleared. He couldn't afford to indulge in longing for a mother he'd never known.

He was there in the wizard's clearing to help the friends that he did know, friends who hadn't abandoned him and walked away. Wildren's plan came back to him.

"Listen, wizard, I will go," he said boldly, "but I want to ask you something first."

Drazagon had reached the caravan. He stopped, and turned round to face Barnabus. "Very well," he replied, grumpily. Clearly, his moods were not to be trusted. "What is it now?"

This was the key moment. It was crucial that Barnabus should give the impression that he was ignorant of the wizard's true intentions. He had to act more convincingly than he'd ever done in his whole life.

"What are you doing here?" he asked innocently.

"Ha! Foolish boy!" retorted the wizard. "Isn't it obvious? Are you so stupid out here in the sticks? Don't you know anything at all about what goes on in Pendarion? That foul brigand Gratzenburg has employed me to destroy the knight who unhorsed him – and his whole family, too. It's not a very respectable job for a wizard of my standing, but he offered me a great deal of gold to do it. And I mean a great deal. I'm regretting it now, as it's proving harder than I'd thought. Still, Gratzenburg is a friend of the king, so it doesn't pay to offend him. Having said that, today is my last day here. I'll make one last attempt, and then I'm going home. I don't care if Gratzenburg is happy or not – he's got his money's worth out of me!"

Barnabus knew that this was his moment. "So you're going to try once more and then go home – whatever the outcome?" he asked.

"Oh, this time I will kill young Elvarin, don't you worry. Just as I killed his father." The wizard said this in such a matter-of-fact way that Barnabus felt like hitting him. Lord Blodrell had always treated Barnabus well. He had to bite his tongue to remain silent. "Then I'll leave, whatever happens," continued the wizard. "I'm not staying in this godforsaken wood any longer. I expect it's all Wildren's fault. He always was a cunning devil." He chuckled.

Barnabus was shocked for the second time that morning. "You know Wildren?" He couldn't imagine two more different people – the murderous Drazagon and the kind, considerate Wildren. How could they possibly know each other?

"Ha. Of course I know Wildren," spat out the wizard. "We were at school and university together. I knew him at the court of old king Tarralast. A more cunning cove you'll never meet. He would have made a fine wizard, too, if he'd turned his mind to it."

"A wizard?" gasped Barnabus. "Wildren is a wizard?" He couldn't believe it.

"You're not listening, boy. I said he **would** have made a fine wizard. He started the training at the same time as me, but he gave it up. He was more interested in politics and diplomacy."

"I think that must have been a different Wildren," said Barnabus, confidently. "The one I know is – well, quite ordinary, really."

Drazagon laughed. It was a loud belly laugh that went on and on. He laughed until the tears ran down his cheeks.

"Well, boy," he said at last, wiping his eyes. "I owe you my thanks! I haven't laughed like that in years! Ordinary? Don't you think for one minute that Wildren is ordinary! He's exactly the opposite!" His manner changed immediately. "Anyway, that's enough gossip. Be off with you. I've got one more spell to cast, and then I'm going home." He turned away from Barnabus once more, and mounted the caravan steps.

Barnabus was now ready to spring his trap. He could pursue Wildren about his past when he got back to the castle - if he got back to the castle.

"Listen," he called out. "I've got to tell you something about Elvarin." He spoke as earnestly as he could.

"I've got no time to listen to any more tales, boy," growled Drazagon over his shoulder. "Be off with you. I've got a spell to cast."

"You must listen," insisted Barnabus. "I'm trying to tell you that you've got the wrong person."

Drazagon turned round to face Barnabus, and came back down the steps. "The wrong person? Don't treat me like an idiot, boy. Gratzenburg wants Elvarin dead because a thousand people saw him knock the old devil off his horse. It's simple revenge. Something I understand well," he added.

"But what if I was to tell you that it wasn't Elvarin? That it was someone else wearing his armour?" Barnabus had cast the bait. He only hoped that this big fish would swallow it.

Drazagon let out another roar of laughter. "If it's true, then Elvarin has more brains than I'd given him credit for." He abruptly stopped laughing and fixed Barnabus with a steely glare. "You mean it, don't you, boy? Don't lie to me! I can tell when you're lying!"

"I'm telling the truth," said Barnabus, maintaining a straight face with difficulty. The fish was hooked. "It wasn't Elvarin who knocked the Black Knight off his horse. Everyone knows he's a useless jouster! Someone else took his place, and Elvarin took the credit!"

Drazagon laughed again. "Good for him! I like the idea of the big buffoon being fooled!" He slapped his knee and laughed once more.

Barnabus knew it was time to pull this fish out of the water. "So you see, you're punishing the wrong person!"

Drazagon's laughter was cut short. "By all that's devilish, you're right, boy. And I can tell you're speaking the truth! Well, well, well, I've been wasting my power on the wrong target! Ha! I've been fooled! Both me and Gratzenburg! That's rich! I quite admire the villain who tricked two old villains like us!" He laughed again.

"So you see," repeated Barnabus, "you're trying to punish the wrong person. You should be concentrating on the real culprit instead."

Drazagon cut short his laughter once more. "Right again, my boy!" He looked at Barnabus with a cunning leer. "I don't suppose you know who that is, do you? I'll let you live if you tell me."

"You've already agreed to do that," Barnabus reminded him.

"Have I? Well, I've changed my mind. Wizard's prerogative. I'll let you live if you tell me who the real culprit is. Remember, I'll know if you're lying!"

"If you kill him, will you go away and leave everyone else alone?"

"I've already told you this is my last attempt, haven't I? I'm leaving, whatever happens. Just tell me who I'm supposed to kill, and then I can do it, and we can all go home."

Barnabus had gone this far; he couldn't turn back now.

I only hope Wildren is right. Otherwise we'll all be dead. Especially me.

"His name is Barnabus. They call him Barnabus Mudpatch, Street Knight of Waxminster." He spoke his own name proudly and clearly. He wanted there to be no mistake.

"A good name and a good title! And an easy one for a magic spell! Is he here as well?"

"Yes. He lives in the castle. He's Elvarin's bodyguard." Barnabus was careful to tell the truth. Drazagon would be suspicious if he detected any lies.

"Good! That makes things nice and simple. Now, let's finish this off, and then we can all get on with our lives! Except for those who are dead, of course," he added.

He strode to the centre of the clearing. As he walked, he seemed to grow bigger with each step. He looked at Barnabus, and he winked.

"Just watch this! It's one of my masterpieces!" He grinned, raising his hands above his head, and pointing his fingers at the sky. "Prepare to be impressed!" he said. Then he began to mumble. Barnabus couldn't hear the words, but he could tell they were having an effect. The tips of Drazagon's fingers began to glow. The mumbling became louder, and the words became audible, but they were in a language that Barnabus didn't understand.

I hope I've got this right, he thought. *I only hope I've got this completely right.*

The tips of Drazagon's fingers glowed brighter and brighter. His face began to shine with the same radiance.

While this was happening the sky began to change. There had been a few pink clouds in the morning sky, reflecting the light of the rising sun, but as soon as Drazagon had begun to chant, more clouds seemed to gather from the horizon. Peculiarly, they were gathering from the horizon in all directions. It was as though all the winds in the world were gathering clouds and sending them to Castle Blodrell.

And not just any clouds. These were dark, sombre storm clouds. Creeping across the heavens like a smothering blanket, they began to block out the light as they converged on the sky above the tall towers of the castle.

In a short time the sky was completely covered, and it was twilight once more, even though it was early in the morning.

Barnabus was amazed and frightened at the same time. The wizard's power was enormous.

Drazagon's voice rose to a shout. He stretched out his hands towards the dense black clouds, and Barnabus heard him cry out, "Barnabus Mudpatch, Street Knight of Waxminster." Immediately, the tips of his fingers burst into flames, and long, straight beams of fire radiated out from his fingers and up into the cloud layer. Ten beams of fire hit the clouds in ten different places, and wherever they touched, the clouds themselves burst into flames.

Drazagon dropped his arms to his sides. His finger tips were no longer glowing.

"Watch this, my boy, and be amazed! Then you'll know why Drazagon is the Crown Wizard of Gothria! This is one of my best spells! Look!"

Barnabus didn't need to be told twice. He was already fascinated by the ten fiery points of flame in the black clouds, and was more than a little scared. He was hoping that Wildren's idea was correct. If not, he was probably doomed. He looked around the clearing, and couldn't see any of the Blodrell Bloodhounds who'd come with him. This meant they were either lying unconscious in the woods, or had fled. Either way, he hoped they were far enough away to not be hurt by whatever happened next.

Now a rumbling sound could be heard. The noise of a full-scale thunderstorm had begun to emanate from the clouds. There was no rain, but thunder was booming, and getting louder. The ten points of flame were spreading out and rapidly approaching each other.

"Now for the finale!" cried Drazagon, his face lit with fanatic glee. "The Black Knight's contract is fulfilled, and I can go home at last!"

He raised his arms so they were pointing out sideways from his body, horizontal and level with his shoulders, and he held them there for a second. "Oh," he said, "and let me show you why you should never trust a wizard. I'm going to destroy the whole castle before your very eyes! Watch!" He lifted his hands and brought them together over his head with a resounding clap.

There was a second's pause, and then everything happened so fast it was impossible for Barnabus to keep track of it all. Lightning burst out of the storm clouds, ten brilliant, jagged bolts of lightning, all at the same time. Drazagon had expected them to strike the castle in search of Barnabus, but of course, nothing of the kind happened. The ten bolts of lightning streaked across the sky, directed not at the castle, but at Barnabus himself, sitting on a log, near Drazagon's caravan. And near Drazagon.

Barnabus just had time to see the look of amazement on Drazagon's face turn to fear as all ten bolts of lightning struck.

And then, everything went black.

Chapter 21

Return to Waxminster

When Barnabus woke up, he was still in the clearing. Everything around him was charred black – the log, the grass, the trees, even the ground itself – and smoke was rising from the remains of the caravan.

There was no sign of Drazagon.

Barnabus was surprised to find that he felt fine. He looked at himself, at his body, his arms and his legs. There was no sign of being struck by lightning. What's more, he felt no pain at all.

He reached inside his tunic and pulled out the medallion. For the first time, the face engraved on it seemed to be smiling. "Thanks, mum," he whispered, and put it back inside his tunic. It was time to go home.

Back in the Library, Barnabus sat with Wildren, Elvarin, Ellie and Captain Draxa for the last time. Wildren was speaking in response to Barnabus's questions.

"Yes, I knew Drazagon as a boy and as a student at the University. You could say we were friends, although Drazagon is not the kind of person to really have friends. But he decided to delve ever deeper into the black arts, and I – I didn't. So we went our separate ways."

"And did you know Sersei? He said she's my mother!" asked Barnabus, eagerly.

"No, I never knew her. Although I knew of her, obviously. She is the most powerful enchantress ever to have lived. Did he really say she's your mother?"

"Yes. He said he let me live just because of her."

"Well, he always had a soft spot for her, even when we were students. Of course, she was much older. As old as the hills, they say. Still, that would explain your own magical protection. Whether you inherited it, or she gave it to you specifically, or it just came from the medallion, I cannot say. But as the son of the most powerful enchantress in history you could be expected to have some magical abilities of your own. Have you ever thought of trying to develop them?" Wildren looked quizzically at Barnabus.

"What do you mean? I don't have any magical abilities!" Barnabus was startled at the idea.

"Well, let it go for now. You are young, and there's plenty of time to develop your talent!"

"I don't know what you ...."

"I said to let it go," interrupted Wildren. "You'll know when the time is right."

"Oh. All right, then." Barnabus was overwhelmed by the new ideas of the last few hours. He couldn't think of himself as the son of an enchantress. He was only happy to have found something out about his mother, the mother he'd never known.

"Is she still alive?" He blurted out. Barnabus couldn't keep the desperation out of his voice.

"Sersei? I expect so. I don't even know if she can die. They say enchantress's don't grow old. No-one knows how old she is. I certainly don't."

"And what about my father? Who was he? Drazagon wouldn't, or couldn't, say. If my mother was so famous, everyone must know my father as well!"

"Well, there were rumours, naturally, but remember, she was welcome anywhere and everywhere. Men fell in love with her all the time – she could enchant them, of course – but as to who she actually loved, well, she kept that to herself. So sadly, I cannot answer your question."

Wildren said this in such a final way it was clear that the subject was closed. Barnabus felt rejected, but he wouldn't give up completely.

"Where's my mother now? If she can live forever, and is so famous, you must know where she is!" He was determined to find out something definite.

"What she does and where she goes is her business alone. Not even kings and emperors can command her. She's a law unto herself. I expect she'll be travelling the world, following her own mysterious ways. It's fortunate, though, that she left you her protection, and such a powerful one at that." Wildren was trying hard to change the subject.

"Yes, I know," said Barnabus, acknowledging defeat at last. "When Drazagon said that the protection she'd given me was at least as good as his, if not better, I knew that I should try your plan. The risk seemed worth taking."

"And you were right," said Captain Draxa.

"Possibly," said Wildren.

"Come on," said Ellie, who'd been silent until now. There'd been such a lot to take in. "The lightning struck Barnabus and Drazagon, and Barnabus was the only survivor. What does that tell us? Drazagon was killed, that's what! And well done, Barnabus, that's what I say." She gave him a big smile, and slapped him on the back.

"Well done Barnabus, indeed," agreed Wildren, "but don't be so sure about Drazagon. He has his own form of protection, and may have just disappeared in order to avoid the lightning rather than have been killed by it."

"Oh no," groaned Elvarin, laying his head on the table. "Then I'm not free of him after all."

"Oh, I think you are. Once again, Barnabus has saved your bacon. Drazagon knows for certain that it wasn't you who knocked the Black Knight off his horse, so he won't pursue you any more. And anyway, he said to Barnabus that this was going to be his last attempt. Even the Black Knight's gold couldn't keep him hunting you forever. He has his pride, you know."

"So, you mean it's over, then?" asked Elvarin, anxiously.

"Yes," said Wildren. Elvarin let out a sigh, and sank back into his chair. "It's over. Life can return to normal here at Castle Blodrell. Well, as normal as it can ever be without Lord Blodrell."

"You're forgetting something, Wildren," said Captain Draxa, quietly.

"Am I? Oh, yes, of course. We do have a Lord Blodrell after all. Forgive me, Elvarin. With all the excitement of hiding you from danger, I'd forgotten that you are now the lord."

"Don't worry, Wildren. I'm not sure I like the idea myself. It smells too much of responsibility to me."

"It'll make you grow up, brother," said Ellie with a smile.

"Yes, we can settle back into some kind of normality, I suppose," said Wildren. "Elvarin must take up the reins of responsibility. Eleanora can go back to the court at Pendarion to complete her education. Captain Draxa can get the castle cleaned up...."

"And what about you, Wildren?" asked Barnabus. "Drazagon gave me the impression that you're more than you seem to be." He smiled at the old man.

"Me? My place is here, assisting Elvarin to become the great lord he is destined to be." Wildren quickly changed the subject. Once more, he didn't like talking about himself. "More to the point, Barnabus, what about you? Would you like to stay here? This is your home, you know. We all owe our lives to you. If that lightning had hit the castle, I'm sure we would all have been killed. Besides, you've become part of our family."

"Go on, boy," said Captain Draxa, with just a touch of emotion in his voice. "I could use you in the Guard."

"What do you mean, in the Guard?" asked Ellie, scornfully. "He's the new Lord Blodrell's bodyguard, that's what he is. Not a common soldier."

"You're right," said Elvarin. "Barnabus, I owe you more than anyone else. It's only because of you that I'm alive at all. Please, stay with us and make your own life here, in whatever way you wish. However you want to live, whatever you want to do, I will make it happen."

Barnabus was surprised at Elvarin's earnestness. He really meant what he said. It only made his decision all the harder. He'd been dreading this moment.

"I want to thank you all for your kindness," he said, "and I'll never forget everything that's happened here. But I have to go home," he added, simply.

"Look, Barnabus," said Elvarin, "you don't have a real home. You live in the streets of Waxminster. You never have enough to eat, and your life is a constant struggle. Stay here. Life is much easier." Elvarin reached out and took his hand. "Stay with us. Please."

Barnabus looked around the table. He knew he would miss them, each and every one. Elvarin, lazy but good humoured. Ellie, the girl warrior with the pretty smile. Captain Draxa, the blunt-talking old soldier. And, of course, Wildren, who'd become the nearest thing to a father he'd ever known.

He looked down at the table, unable to meet their eyes. "It's no good," he said. "I've got to go home. That's just how it is."

Ellie and Elvarin started to speak again, but Wildren interrupted them. "Don't worry, Barnabus. If you must go, you must go. We won't hold it against you. Only you must know that you will always be welcome here, and that if ever you need anything from us – anything at all – you only need to ask and it will be yours."

"I know," said Barnabus. "And I can't thank you enough for everything you've done for me. But now it's over, and I must go."

"Of course, my dear boy. And so it will be."

"When will you leave, Barnabus?" asked Ellie, sadly.

"Tomorrow morning," he said. "Early."

And so the next morning, Barnabus found himself on a cart, not dissimilar from the one that had brought him to Blodrell Sonnet in the first place. He hadn't wanted to return to Waxminster in a grand carriage – which is what Wildren had offered – because, as he said, "It would only draw attention, and I want to sneak in quietly."

The company on the journey was better this time, though. Two of the Blodrell Bloodhounds – Loral and Gladric – had offered to take him. They claimed they had a delivery of vegetables to make, but Barnabus thought that might just have been an excuse.

It was a two-day journey, but it seemed much shorter than that. Gladric steered the horses most of the time, while Loral taught Barnabus how to whittle. After carving a spoon and then a fork out of pieces of wood, he showed him how to make a simple flute. It was enough to play tunes on as they sat round the campfire at night.

Gladric was a born storyteller, and kept them enthralled with his tales of dragons, demons and trolls. He was also a very good cook, and had brought plenty of provisions for their journey. The weather was so fine that they could sleep out under the stars at night, without any need for the tent they'd brought.

The only shadow for Barnabus was the sadness he felt at leaving his friends behind.

When the cart departed from Castle Blodrell, there'd been quite a crowd to see him off. Not only had Wildren, Elvarin and Ellie been there, but Captain Draxa had assembled the entire castle guard to line the road from the castle all the way to Blodrell Sonnet. And there, in the village, a crowd had gathered too. He recognised many of the Blodrell Bloodhounds, and every door and window was packed with waving villagers.

The word had leaked out that it was Barnabus who'd saved the life of the new Lord Blodrell, and prevented the whole castle from being destroyed by lightning. It was rumoured that he'd beaten a wizard in a duel, although few people believed it. Whatever the truth was, there was no doubt in anyone's mind that Barnabus was a true celebrity, and should be treated like one.

It was Wildren he thought most about. Ellie as well, of course, but Wildren gave him the most cause for thought. "Why were you so confident, Wildren? You know, before the flame demon attacked, you said you didn't want to fix a plan, that everything would work out. What did you mean?"

"I meant that you would solve every problem that arose. And I was right."

"Me?"

"Yes, you. I didn't need to make a plan. I've had total faith in you since the beginning, and I was right. You are a special boy, Barnabus, very special. I knew you'd think of something every time, and you did."

Barnabus roused himself from the pleasant memories to see the tall towers of Waxminster before him. They'd arrived. The wagon slowly rolled over the massive drawbridge, and approached the main gate. The Gate Watch saw nothing unusual in a cart full of vegetables driven by country lads. It was market day, after all, so they waved them through without stopping.

The transition happened so quickly that Barnabus hardly noticed it. One minute he was outside the city walls on a quiet country road, and the next he was in a crowded marketplace.

The sounds and smells assaulted him from all sides. It was a far cry from the gentle pace of life in

Blodrell Sonnet and the peace and quiet of the countryside.

All of his senses told him that he was back in Waxminster,

Then, without any warning, he heard a whooshing sound, and a mud ball hit him on the back of the head. Loral and Gladric burst into peals of laughter, but Barnabus was furious. He span round to see who'd thrown it, and heard a slimy voice coming from a gloomy alleyway.

"Welcome home, Barney boy."

"Spider?" he called out, angrily. "Is that you?" He raised his fists, ready for a fight.

"Course it's me! Who did you think it was? Wagsnatch? He couldn't hit a barn door at five paces." A snigger could be heard coming from the alleyway.

"Hey, Spider," Barnabus called out, a broad grin spreading across his face. "I've missed you too!"

It was good to be back.

About the Author

As well as being a writer, Steve Moran is a musician, storyteller, puppeteer, actor and scientist.

When not involved in any of these things he loves to read about history. That's where he got the idea for this book. He hopes that you enjoy it, and learn to love history too!

Steve lives with his wife and son in Sussex, England.

Printed in Great Britain
by Amazon.co.uk, Ltd.,
Marston Gate.